ISAAC ASIMOV'S
ROBOTS
IN TIME

by
WILLIAM F. WU

THE LAWS OF ROBOTICS

1.

A robot may not injure a human being, or through inaction, allow a human being to come to harm.

2.

A robot must obey the orders given it by human beings except where such orders would conflict with the First Law.

3.

A robot must protect its own existence as long as such protection does not conflict with the First or Second Law.

Other AvoNova Books in
ISAAC ASIMOV'S ROBOTS IN TIME *Series*
by William F. Wu

PREDATOR
MARAUDER
WARRIOR
DICTATOR
EMPEROR

ISAAC ASIMOV'S
ROBOTS
IN TIME™

INVADER

WILLIAM F. WU

Databank by Matt Elson

A Byron Preiss Book

AVON BOOKS • NEW YORK

ISAAC ASIMOV'S ROBOTS IN TIME: INVADER is an original publication of Avon Books. This work has never before appeared in book form. This work is a novel. Any similarity to actual persons or events is purely coincidental.

An Isaac Asimov's Robot City book.

AVON BOOKS
A division of
The Hearst Corporation
1350 Avenue of the Americas
New York, New York 10019

First AvoNova Printing: September 1994

AVONOVA TRADEMARK REG. U.S. PAT. OFF. AND IN OTHER COUNTRIES, MARCA REGISTRADA, HECHO EN U.S.A.

Printed in the U.S.A.

RA 10 9 8 7 6 5 4 3 2 1

*This novel is dedicated to
the memory of my maternal grandmother,
Mae Franking,
who passed her English and Scottish
descent to me and became the
first novelist in the family.*

Special thanks are due during the time of writing this novel to Dr. William Q. Wu and Cecile F. Wu, my parents, for indulging my lifelong interest in history; Ricia Mainhardt; Bridgett and Marty Marquardt; Michael D. Toman; and John Betancourt, Leigh Grossman, Keith R. A. DeCandido, and Byron Preiss.

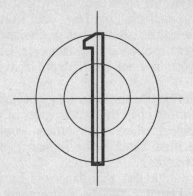

R. Hunter, a humaniform robot, waited as Steve Chang looked up at him angrily. They stood in the small office of Mojave Center Governor, in the underground city of Mojave Center. Steve began to pace.

"I hardly slept at all, Hunter," Steve growled. "Jane could be anywhere in the world, at any time in history. That's the toughest kidnapping to solve anyone could imagine. We have to start looking for her. Once we get going, I'll get back to normal."

"You know that R. Ishihara cannot allow her to be harmed under the First Law of Robotics," said Hunter. "That will not change, no matter where they are."

"I know, I know—'A robot may not injure a human being, or, through inaction, allow a human being to come to harm,' " Steve droned impatiently. "But Ishihara is working for Wayne Nystrom, renegade roboticist," said Steve. "That tells us how great Ishihara's judgment must be. I don't trust him to follow the First Law responsibly."

"Dr. Nystrom apparently convinced Ishihara to help him under the First Law," said Hunter. "Once he had done that, Ishihara had no choice but to obey him under the Second Law. However, Ishihara will protect both Jane and Dr. Nystrom from immediate harm."

"So who cares if the Second Law of Robotics says, 'A robot must obey the orders given it by human beings except where such orders would conflict with the First Law,' if the human giving orders can't be trusted?"

"I do not predict that Jane will be with them long," said Hunter. "Wayne Nystrom will be searching for MC 6 in the same time and place we will. That narrows the search for Jane considerably. Our search for MC 6 will take us to them."

"Well, we know about when and where to find them, then," said Steve. "So let's go!"

"Not so fast." Hunter turned and eased his body into the desk chair.

"Why not?"

"We must prepare this mission with the same care we used in the others. Since we are going back to fifth-century Britain, I will retain my present appearance. It is consistent with the gene pool of the local people we will meet." A brawny six feet six inches tall with short blond hair and blue eyes, Hunter had been designed with the ability to change his shape and appearance at will.

"All right, *fine*. That's your department; it won't matter to me. What else do we have to do?" Steve put both fists on his hips and glared at Hunter. "I've already taken the vaccines you arranged this morning. I assume you've prepared period clothing, just as you did before."

"Yes. I took the clothing to the Bohung Institute while you were trying to sleep. However, I have hired Harriet Lane, a new historian, to join us."

"Well, where is she?"

"She is due here in a few minutes; I arranged for her to receive her vaccines from R. Cushing, the medical robot who tended your head injury after our fourth mission. Together, we will have to decide how to explain your Chinese descent to Britons who have never heard of China or seen anyone of your race and ethnicity."

"Well, we told the ancient Germans in Roman times that I was a slave from the eastern Mediterranean. That should be good enough."

"Perhaps. My internal clock says the time is 7:38 P.M. While we wait for Harriet, I must report to the Governor Robot Oversight Committee."

"All right, I'll shut up." Steve folded his arms across his chest and continued pacing anxiously. "I just hope she shows up soon."

Nodding, Hunter called the the city computer and instructed it to contact the four members of the Governor Robot Oversight Committee for him. Then he waited while they were located for the conference call. In front of him, Steve still stomped back and forth across the small room.

Hunter could not avoid making reports to the Oversight Committee. He had been designed and built specifically for the committee in order to search for Mojave Center Governor, one of six experimental gestalt robots who were supposed to be running certain cities. All the other Governor robots had mysteriously shut themselves down. However, MC Governor had suddenly divided into the six component gestalt humaniform robots out of which he was comprised and vanished. No one knew why.

Dr. Wayne Nystrom, an eccentric roboticist, had designed and built the Governor robots. However, the Governor Robot Oversight Committee had been studying their performance and judging their efficiency. When the Governors began to fail, Wayne Nystrom had apparently felt that his career was in danger. He had been trying to beat Hunter to each of the component robots of MC Governor in order to dismantle and examine them for the mysterious flaw that had shut down the first five Governors before Hunter could reassemble MC Governor and turn him over to the Oversight Committee to complete their study.

When Hunter had arrived in Mojave Center, he had learned that MC Governor had modified an existing piece of technology in the Bohung Institute into a time travel device. Then each of his component robots had miniaturized themselves to microscopic size and fled back in time to a different era, intending to hide forever. Jane believed their motivation was the Third Law of Robotics, "A robot must protect its own existence as long as such protection does not conflict with the First or Second Law." Unknown to them, however, a flaw in the miniaturization caused each of them to return to full size at different times, wherever they happened to be.

At that point, they had to masquerade as human. Two dangers presented themselves as a result. The first was that they could alter the direction of history by living throughout the centuries and causing people to act in different ways, driven by the Three

Laws of Robotics. Hunter had to prevent that in order to avoid harm to all humans by having the timeline of history significantly changed.

In addition, when the component robots or their material remains reached the approximate time they had left, they exploded with nuclear force. As Hunter prepared to go back with his team to find MC 6, he also was monitoring the news broadcasts of a mysterious nuclear explosion in south-central England. Only his team members knew that it had been caused by MC 6 exploding.

Now Wayne had a robot named R. Ishihara helping him. Originally, Hunter had instructed Ishihara to apprehend Wayne if he returned from the past to the time travel sphere in Room F-12 of the Bohung Institute. Somehow, the roboticist had used an argument involving the Three Laws of Robotics to induce Ishihara to cooperate with him.

On five separate missions, Hunter had led his team of humans in pursuit of the other five component robots. All five had been caught. Now they were here in the office of MC Governor, where they stood merged and shut down, waiting for the last component robot in order to complete MC Governor again. Once he had been put back together, the Oversight Committee would investigate why the other Governors had shut down and why MC Governor had divided and fled.

Hunter had reported to the Governor Robot Oversight Committee on his progress after each mission. However, he felt that the existence of time travel held incalculable potential harm for all humans. For that reason, he had kept it a secret from all except the humans and robots whose help he required.

Certainly if the scientists on the Oversight Committee learned of the time travel, it would never remain a secret. The discovery would be too valuable for a committee of scientists to ignore. Wayne Nystrom had discovered MC Governor's development of time travel on his own, before Hunter had learned of it. Hunter could not do anything about that.

"Hunter, city computer calling. The Governor Robot Oversight Committee is ready for your conference call."

"Thank you. Please connect me."

As before, the faces of the four committee members appeared on Hunter's internal video screen in split portrait shots from their various locations. Everyone exchanged greetings. Then Hunter began his report.

"The first five component robots are in custody and merged," said Hunter.

"That's great," said Dr. Redfield, the tall blonde. "I suppose this has been an easy assignment for you. You began less than two weeks ago."

"I must repeat once again that past success does not predict the difficulty of the final mission," said Hunter. "As always, I cannot promise that the remainder of my work will be completed within a similar period of time."

"Where did this mission take place?" Dr. Chin asked. "Previously, you have reported quite a wide range of locations around the world."

"In northern China," said Hunter. "On the border of Mongolia." He remained deliberately vague in his reports. So far, his reserve had forestalled persistent questioning from the committee members.

"Northern China." Professor Post nodded, idly stroking his black beard for a moment. "Well, that's interesting. Do you have a lead on MC 6?"

"I must investigate the British Isles," said Hunter. "This is preliminary information."

"Which one?" Dr. Chin asked.

"I shall begin in England. On previous missions, a certain amount of travel has been involved."

"Wait a minute," said Dr. Chin. "Haven't you heard about the big explosion? Won't that interfere with your search?"

"I will take it into account as I make my plans," said Hunter.

"Do you think MC 6 may have been destroyed in the explosion?" Professor Post asked calmly.

"It is an inescapable consideration," said Hunter. "However, I can only proceed and find what I may."

"I am not surprised," said Dr. Khanna, in his Hindi accent. "However, your work has been completed very quickly to date. We are all impressed."

"I must repeat that I can make no guarantee of my schedule to come," said Hunter.

"Yes, I heard you the first time," said Dr. Khanna, with a trace of annoyance in his tone. "You repeat that warning in every report. However, you continue to complete each mission in the same length of time. What would make this final mission any different?"

"The explosion, and its after-effects," said Dr. Redfield. "He may have a harder time now."

"My original point remains valid," said Hunter. "I have no prediction about the challenges that my team will face. Anything can happen." Hunter realized that he had made a mistake. Before, he had never told the committee members that he was going to an area where a nuclear explosion had occurred.

"We note your caution," said Dr. Chin. "And as always, we wish you good luck."

"That will be fine, Hunter," said Dr. Redfield. "I suggest we allow you to get to work."

"Thank you," said Hunter. "I am ready to begin. Do you have any final questions?"

No one did.

"Good luck," said Dr. Chin.

"Thank you. Good-bye." Hunter broke the connection and turned to Steve, speaking aloud. "Report completed."

"Good!" Steve glanced impatiently at the closed door of the office. "So where's our historian?"

"I expect her at any time."

"All right, all right. What do we do in the meantime? Do we know what MC 6's specialty was, within MC Governor's responsibilities? Jane always seemed to think that was important."

"I have that information," said Hunter. "The data the committee originally gave me about MC Governor provides the original divisions of expertise among the gestalt robots. Since Jane correctly identified the specialties of the first five component robots, I know by process of elimination that MC 6 is the portion of MC Governor that specialized in maintaining social stability among humans."

"Yeah? What does that mean, exactly?"

"In Mojave Center, that meant keeping track of various human needs, not only for survival and protection from harm, but for emotional satisfaction: leisure pursuits, choices of education and career, and career organization to encourage challenges and accomplishments."

"Okay. But Jane also used to guess that a component robot's choice of where to hide related to his specialty in Mojave Center."

"Yes, I remember. Using the same sort of logic Jane expressed prior to earlier missions, I surmise that MC 6 therefore deliberately fled with the question of social instability in mind. However, England is an unusual case; since 1066, it has had a relatively high degree of stability for an Old World nation, despite some occasional turbulence. However, I calculate that MC 6 will return to his full human size from miniaturization in the late fifth century, in a time of extreme social turmoil and political instability. Since he did not plan that, the timing is ironic, to say the least."

Steve started to answer. When he heard footsteps approaching the office, he stopped and glanced at Hunter, who nodded. Steve opened the door.

"Oh—you startled me." Harriet smiled and came in as Steve stepped back. She was tall and slender, about forty years old, with short, wavy brown hair.

Hunter introduced them. "Harriet specializes in late Roman and post-Roman Britain."

"I love the period," Harriet said cheerfully. "And I've had my dinner and my vaccinations, as you instructed. What comes next?"

"Have you both successfully taken your sleep courses in ancient British and Latin?" Hunter asked.

"Yes," said Harriet. "I was familiar with both languages, but the course will help me speak them."

"I took the British, too," said Steve. "And I updated the Latin from our third mission because

Hunter said it had changed some in the centuries that had passed. But what is this British language, anyhow? Did it turn into English later?"

"Not really," said Harriet. "It's the language that was spoken in Britain before the Romans arrived, and it coexisted with Latin during their occupation. It later evolved into Welsh, Cornish, and Breton. But what we call English was based originally on Anglo-Saxon and Norman French."

"But we'll still need the Latin this time, too?" Steve asked.

"We'll find a lot of Latin in the time we're visiting," said Harriet. "But it doesn't stay for many more years. Except for some monasteries and place names, Latin disappears and then reenters English again much later."

"Oh. Shows what I know about it." Steve turned to Hunter. "Have you told Harriet about Wayne and Ishihara? How they're trying to beat us to MC 6 and why?"

"Yes, he has," said Harriet. "He also told me that they kidnapped your friend Jane on your last mission. I'm sure you're worried about her."

"Well, yeah. That's true." Steve looked at Hunter. "Can we go yet?"

"We will go to the Bohung Institute. The Security vehicle is waiting outside."

"Good."

Hunter drove them through the calm, clean streets of the underground city. Steve sat next to Harriet, too tense to speak. The electric motor of the vehicle hummed softly as they drove by humans and robots on their daily routines who were unaware that the secret of time travel, with all its potential danger to change history, lay in their midst.

Before the first mission, Hunter had closed the Bohung Institute. He had arranged for a detail of Security robots to guard it. They allowed his team inside, of course, and they walked to Room F-12.

Steve looked around the familiar room. Room F-12 was a large facility that housed an opaque sphere about fifteen meters in diameter. With its console, the sphere could both miniaturize humans and robots to microscopic size and also send them back through time, in either normal or microscopic condition. Countertops lined the rest of the room, filled with computers, monitors, a communication console, and miscellaneous office equipment.

Hunter introduced Harriet to R. Daladier, a robot he had left in the room to apprehend Wayne Nystrom and Ishihara if they returned unexpectedly.

Steve waited anxiously, knowing the team would have to discuss the mission further and change clothes before Hunter would actually take them back in time.

"I arranged to have period costumes made for us earlier today," said Hunter. He pointed to four neatly folded stacks of clothing on one counter. Four sets of leather boots stood next to them. "Please check them for authenticity. No synthetics have been used."

"I see four outfits," said Steve. "We only have three of us this time."

"We will take a full costume for Jane," said Hunter. "I expect to find her, but she may need period clothing. She left China in the time of Kublai Khan wearing a robe and trousers from that culture."

"Right."

Harriet lifted a long, brown tunic and shook it out. "Tunics for you two. Wool, of course; that's right. A rope belt. Loosely cut, longer than knee-length. It looks fine." She lifted another. "This white undertunic is made of cotton. It was expensive in ancient Britain. A sign of prosperity. And I see the shift I will wear under my wool gown is also made of cotton."

"Underclothing of cotton will be far more comfortable for you two than wool, fur, or any other acceptable choice," said Hunter. "I believe the comfort will increase your efficiency. Besides, suggesting a hint of prosperity can be part of the roles we will play."

"As you decide." Harriet lifted her gown, also of brown wool. "Full-length, loose, and blousy . . . long sleeves. Yes, this will be fine, too."

"What about the boots?" Steve asked.

Harriet picked up one of them. "About these roles, Hunter. What are they?"

"From the historical data I have taken from the city library, I suggest that I play the role of a horse trader from Gaul. You two will masquerade as my wife and servant. Unless you find a flaw in this plan, I would like to say that I wish to move away from the crumbling, unstable Roman Empire in Gaul and raise my horse herds in Britain."

"Go on." She put down the first boot and studied another one.

"I learned that southern England in this time has ideal horse-grazing land and that Artorius, the man upon whom the legend of King Arthur was based, led a troop of cavalry. He would have to be concerned about a reliable source of mounts for his men."

"Hold it," said Steve, grinning in spite of his eagerness to get on their way. "We aren't taking any horses with us. You can't horse-trade without them."

"I propose to say that I am looking for land in Britain before bringing my herd over the Channel," said Hunter. "Would this sound reasonable?"

"The boots are acceptable, too." Harriet paused thoughtfully as she put the last boot down. "Yes, your story will be plausible, though you could improve on it. However, bringing something to trade would be more convincing. You could be an ironworker, a trader in silver, a soldier . . . the list of possibilities is very long."

"I chose the role after due consideration," said Hunter. "I must play a role that will carry some prestige without having to take material objects into the past. We must take some coins and our clothing, but every item we take increases the chance of influencing history in a way we do not intend and cannot predict. The role of soldier might put Steve into greater danger than I would prefer."

"Ah—you're a believer in chaos theory as applied to the events of history." She smiled, amused.

"I no longer believe in the most pure and extreme form of chaos theory," said Hunter. "My team has made five missions into the past without altering our own time in any way that I can detect."

"Good. Then you're coming around to my way of thinking about this."

"Not entirely," said Hunter. "I tell each historian I hire that I do not know where the threshold of significant change lies. If I can go into the past as a horse trader so that we do not have to take any merchandise with us, then we take the least risk."

"I do not believe in it at all," said Harriet, casually. "But you're the boss. I accept your priorities."

"I still say a horse trader would take horses with him," said Steve. "Even just one stallion to show off. The people we see are going to expect that."

"We can claim we brought a couple of horses that were lost in a storm as we sailed across the Channel," said Harriet. "That was not unheard-of in these times."

"Am I correct in concluding that Artorius must value the source of his mounts?" Hunter asked.

"Oh, yes. The single greatest advantage the Britons have over the Saxons is their training in Roman cavalry strategy and tactics. You see, the Saxons in this time are unmounted but numerous. Artorius had to keep his men supplied with good, healthy horses."

"Good," said Hunter. He pointed to three cloth pouches on the counter. "We also have a small pouch of coins from this period for each of us to carry."

"Late Roman coins?" She pulled one open and drew out one of the coins. "Since we will claim to have come from Gaul, that would be our currency. Britain primarily still uses the same, but some native coins had to be minted, too."

"Our coins are all late Roman. Also, we have a small bag for Steve to carry. It contains a change of underclothing for each of you and some bread, cheese, and dried meat. I do not know how long it will take us to find food for you."

"It shouldn't be too hard," said Harriet. "Southern England remained heavily Romanized culturally and densely populated for many years after the Romans left Britain on its own."

Steve picked up the bag and looked inside. "Okay. I'll put Jane's clothes and boots in here."

"I will prepare the console. Please take turns changing your clothes in the next room."

Steve waited while Harriet changed first. Hunter walked to the console that controlled the sphere and altered the settings. Steve began to pace again.

"Are you taking us back at night again?" Steve asked, glancing up at Hunter. "Since we're leaving in the evening?"

"I feel this works best," said Hunter. "We arrive in near-darkness to avoid notice."

"I'd rather go back in daylight so we can start looking for Jane right away."

"You will be ready to sleep in several more hours," said Hunter. "If we go back at a time that conflicts with your own sleep schedule, then you and Harriet will be inefficient. Matching your schedule to arrive in daylight would now require waiting until tomorrow morning to leave."

"Well—forget it, then. Let's just go."

Harriet returned from the other room, wearing her long gown and leather boots. "How do I look?"

"Very authentic," said Hunter.

Harriet laughed lightly. "I don't think that's what I was asking, but thanks, anyway."

Steve grinned but said nothing as he went to change in the adjoining room. He emerged wearing the long tunics and boots, which felt similar to the tunic he had worn to ancient Germany in Roman times.

"The console is ready," said Hunter. "Harriet, you should know that I have the belt unit that will trigger it, even from the time to which we are going. After we arrive, I will carry it in a hollow space within my torso."

"All right." Harriet nodded, tugging at her gown to straighten it over her rope belt. "Hunter, when we first discussed the mission, you told me we would visit the site of the archaeological dig now known as Cadbury Castle in the time of Artorius. How about telling us now *exactly* when in time our destination is?"

"And tell me where Cadbury Castle is," Steve added. "I'm still in the dark."

"Cadbury Castle lies in Somerset, in central southern England," said Hunter. "The modern town of South Cadbury lies immediately to the north. Farther north, but within sight, is the city of Glastonbury. We will arrive on the evening of April 21, in A.D. 459."

Steve grinned. "I still don't know where we're going, except that we'll be in England."

"It won't be the England most people think of," said Harriet. "The Roman Empire left Britain to fend for itself against invading barbarians in A.D. 410. The same Celtic tribes who lived there before the Romans arrived still remained, but now they had a strong Roman cultural and military influence. By A.D. 459, when we'll arrive, the Britons will have been resisting the Saxons who had invaded and settled along the Humber and Wash rivers in southeastern Britain for half a century. The failing Roman Empire still just barely exists across the English Channel in Gaul."

"I think I got the gist of that." Steve shrugged, still grinning.

"I'm sure we'll all manage just fine."

Hunter opened the sphere. He helped Harriet climb inside first. By this time, the routine was familiar to Steve; as always, he slid down the curved interior surface to the bottom, where Harriet already sat. Hunter climbed in, closing the sphere after him to leave them in darkness.

Jane Maynard landed with a thump on wet grass. A cold drizzle fell from a dark, overcast sky. She pushed herself up and brushed her long, brown hair out of her eyes. Wayne Nystrom got up on her right; Ishihara, still holding her right arm in one hand, remained on her left.

"Foul weather," Wayne muttered.

"Where are we now?" Jane demanded. A few moments ago by subjective measuring, Wayne and Ishihara had forcibly taken her away from the palace grounds of Kublai Khan in thirteenth-century China. First, to escape Hunter, they had simply jumped a few hours ahead, to the peasant village where they had been staying. Then Wayne had taken a few moments to reset his belt unit before bringing them here, wherever it was.

"We're in Britain, two-thirty in the afternoon of April 19, A.D. 459," said Wayne.

Ishihara stood, then helped Jane to her feet. "This cool, damp weather is potentially harmful to humans. We must find shelter for you, especially before nightfall."

Jane looked around, tugging her Chinese robe tightly around her. Beneath it, she also wore matching baggy trousers. Shepherds sat huddled under trees in the distance, surrounded by their flocks in the drizzle; none were looking this way. Most of the terrain was open, rolling grassland, with clumps of trees scattered here and there. Some tilled fields lay among them, with young shoots too small to identify from here. In the distance, she could see two high hills, one much farther away than the other. A small village lay on the plateau of the nearer hill, and an outer wall of earth and wood surrounded its base.

"That's why I brought us here in the middle of the afternoon," said Wayne. "We have some time before sundown." He smiled suddenly. "We have even more time before Hunter gets here."

"What do you mean?" Ishihara asked.

"I guess it doesn't matter if Jane hears this. I estimate that MC 6 will return to his full size in a couple of days. Hunter has repeatedly arrived within twenty-four hours of the time when the component robots return to normal size." Wayne handed the belt unit to Ishihara.

"What about it?" Jane asked casually, as though the point meant nothing. She watched Ishihara put the belt unit inside his Chinese peasant blouse. Then, under the cloth, he opened his torso and hid the unit inside.

"Therefore, we should have a few days to learn our way around, establish some contacts, and be prepared for both MC 6 and Hunter's team before they arrive." Wayne shook his head. "I should have tried this before, but in places like a buccaneer town and the Russian front in World War II, I didn't want to stay any longer than I had to. And in the dinosaur age and in ancient Germany, I hadn't figured it out yet."

"But you planned to make friends with those peasants in China?" Jane asked.

"No, it just worked out that way," said Wayne. "But now, when Hunter arrives, he must consider your welfare, too. Combining some earlier preparations with that problem for him gives me the best chance I have had yet. Ishihara, I instruct you to shut off your radio reception now and keep it off until I order otherwise."

Jane understood. When Hunter arrived, he might attempt to communicate directly with Ishihara. Wayne did not want any communication between them.

Wayne looked around. "Ishihara, suggest where we should go."

"I propose we walk to the nearest peasant hut." He pointed to a hut from which a narrow, lazy trail of smoke drifted low in the air. A narrow road meandered among the hills, passing by the hut. "Before we can communicate with more than gestures, I will have to begin learning the local language. If the response is hostile, we can walk along the road to meet someone else, perhaps in that village."

"Maybe we should try the village first. That looks a more likely place for MC 6 to show up."

"A village offers more potential harm, as well," said Ishihara. "If we can find lodging elsewhere, then we can visit the village later."

"Yeah, okay."

Ishihara led them through the drizzle toward the hut he had chosen. He did not bother to take Jane's arm. She walked behind him, with Wayne next to her.

Jane knew Ishihara had no reason to fear she would run away from them right now. Until she knew that Hunter and Steve had arrived, and where they were, she had nowhere to go. She would certainly be safer in Ishihara's company than anywhere else here, and she saw no chance she could get the belt unit out of Ishihara's torso.

For now, she would just have to bide her time.

As they approached the hut, Jane could smell bread baking. She was not hungry, but she liked the familiar aroma. A donkey grazing behind the hut stopped and looked up at them. Near it, a small farm wagon had been left under a tree. The entire scene made the locale seem less strange.

"Hold it," said Wayne, stopping. "Does anybody know what language they speak here?"

"No," said Ishihara.

Jane said nothing. She blinked drizzle out of her eyes and rubbed her arms together.

"My history isn't too good," said Wayne. "Are the Romans still here?"

"The Roman Empire ceased to defend Britain in A.D. 410," said Ishihara.

"If the Romans left, I suppose no one speaks Latin here any more," said Wayne. "I took that sleep course in Latin for that trip to Roman Germany. You accessed Latin then, too. Maybe some people here still speak it."

"We can make an attempt to communicate with Latin," said Ishihara.

Jane had also taken the Latin sleep course before the mission to ancient Germany. Since Wayne and Ishihara did not ask her about it, however, she chose not to volunteer the fact. She had no specific plan in mind, but keeping her facility with Latin a secret seemed like a good idea.

"Please go first," Wayne said to Ishihara.

"Of course." Ishihara walked toward the front door of the hut.

Suddenly a couple of dogs barked in the distance behind them. Ishihara stopped and turned. Jane looked, also, and saw two shepherds hurrying down a nearby hill from their flock of sheep. Their dogs, both large and black, ran ahead of them.

"We must wait here," said Ishihara quickly. "Do not alarm the dogs by moving suddenly. I will speak to the men when they reach us."

A woman came to the door of the hut. Four children peered from around her long, full skirt made of some rough cloth. The youngest was a toddler, the eldest maybe ten or eleven years old. None of them spoke. All of them stared cautiously at the strangers.

"It's our clothes, I guess," Said Wayne quietly. "Jane has a fancy Chinese robe and pants and we have Chinese peasant outfits. We'll never explain them."

"Maybe we can use the clothes to our advantage," said Jane. "I'm richly dressed by peasant standards. They may be afraid of us as strangers, but they might not want to turn away an important lady. And only our clothing is strange. We looked more out of place in China, no matter what kind of clothes we wore."

"Well, that's true," Wayne said slowly. He turned

to study her face. "But why are you so willing to cooperate all of a sudden?"

"I need food and shelter as much as you do. We can't just spend the next few days standing out in the rain."

"Yeah."

Suddenly the two dogs ran up, still barking. They dodged and danced around, cautious but not attacking. Jane slowly extended one hand for them to sniff. Instead, they both jumped back.

"I suggest we masquerade as a wealthy lady and her two servants," said Ishihara.

"Whatever you think will work," said Wayne.

"We are fortunate to have no weapons," said Ishihara. "We will appear as less of a danger."

As the shepherds drew near, they slowed to a walk. Jane saw that one was only twelve or thirteen years old. The other appeared to be his father.

Ishihara greeted them in Latin, speaking in a formal tone. "Good day. We are strangers here, seeking shelter from the rain."

The shepherd showed no sign of understanding him. He nodded politely and said something they could not understand. Then he waited expectantly.

Ishihara lifted his hand, feeling the drizzle, and spoke in Latin again. "We would like to have shelter from the rain, at least for a short time." He gestured toward the hut and patted his abdomen. "If you can spare any small amount of food, it would be very welcome."

The shepherd nodded, speaking again, and pointed to the village on top of the hill in the distance.

"He wants us to go to the village." Ishihara continued speaking in Latin, since Wayne and Jane both understood him. "I do not see how we can force ourselves on this family without causing them harm."

"They must be more scared than they seem," said Jane.

"We don't have any money to pay for food," said Wayne. "Or a place to stay."

"Maybe Ishihara can do chores in exchange for hospitality." Jane glanced around. Behind the hut, she saw a small stack of cut firewood and a loose pile of uncut tree branches near it. Some unsplit logs lay scattered around. "Here—tell him I have a bad leg."

"Huh?" Wayne looked at her.

Jane turned toward the woman in the doorway. With a hopeful smile, Jane patted her leg under her long robe and took a limping step toward the hut. The peasant woman looked down and suddenly shooed her children out of the way and gestured to Jane to come inside.

As Jane feigned a limp to the doorway, her hostess pulled a small, three-legged stool forward. She took Jane's arm and helped her to the stool, speaking in a soothing tone. Jane sat down out of the drizzle but just inside the hut, where she could see the others.

Her husband watched cautiously for a moment, not speaking. Then his wife spoke sharply to him. He nodded and spoke to his eldest son. The boy nodded and plodded back up the hill toward the flock of sheep, calling one of the dogs to follow him. The other dog walked to Jane, its tail wagging, and sniffed her hand.

"The man's not going to leave the hut while we're

here, is he?" Wayne grinned. "I guess I wouldn't, either. But now what do we do?"

"Ishihara, cut some wood for them," Jane said quietly. "Don't ask about it, because I think hospitality will force them to decline your offer. Just begin."

"I do not see an ax or any other tool to use," said Ishihara, looking around the small pile of wood that was already cut.

Jane looked around the hut. "I can see some axes just inside the door here."

Ishihara leaned inside, picked up a long-handled ax, and carried it to the uncut wood. Without a word, he picked up an unsplit log and began to split it. The shepherd watched him for a moment, then walked to the doorway. He picked up another ax and joined Ishihara.

"I guess he figures if he can't tend the sheep, he might as well get something done," said Wayne.

The peasant woman stood over Jane and spoke. From her tone and facial expression, Jane felt she was asking a question, but none of her words meant anything to Jane. All Jane could do was shrug helplessly.

"Ygerna." The woman pointed to herself.

"Oh—your name is Ygerna?" Jane touched her own chest with her finger. "Jane."

"Jane."

"Yes." Jane nodded, smiling.

Her hostess knelt and patted her own leg where Jane had indicated her leg was sore. She spoke again, asking the same question as before. When Jane shrugged apologetically, Ygerna stood up and went outside.

"Would they object if I came in out of the rain?"

Wayne asked. "I don't want to mess up a good situation, but I guess they do have the idea that you're important and we're your servants."

"I think you're right." Jane smiled. "Come on in. We'll see what she does. As long as we're considerate, I think we'll be all right."

Wayne came inside the hut. He squatted down across the doorway from Jane.

The children stared at both of them, whispering among themselves, but they focused most of their attention on Jane's Chinese robe.

Ygerna bustled back inside, holding what appeared to be two handfuls of mud, grass, and other plants. She carried this mixture to the back of the hut, where she knelt with her back to Jane. Her children gathered around her, watching to see what she was going to do.

As Ygerna knelt in front of a narrow brick fireplace on the far side from the door, Jane looked around the hut for the first time. A portion of the hut had been sectioned off by a curtain hanging from the ceiling. Since she could see small sleeping pallets on the near side of the fireplace, she guessed that the curtain hid their parents' pallet. One rough wooden table stood in the center of the room, with wooden stools around it. Above the fire, a small metal door was inset into the chimney. Ygerna poured water from an earthenware pitcher into a metal pot and hung it on a hook over the fire.

A few minutes later, Ygerna stirred the mud packs into the steaming, small metal pot. Then she carried the pot to Jane and knelt at her feet. Her children followed her but hung back slightly, still watching with fascination.

Ygerna gently moved Jane's robe back over the

leg Jane had pretended was hurting her. Carefully, Ygerna slipped the leg of Jane's trousers up.
As Jane watched in silence, Ygerna straightened
her leg slightly and then began to smear the mud
poultice on it. Jane realized that the purpose of this
treatment, aside from any superstition the culture
might have, was to apply and hold the heat against
her injury.

Feeling trapped, Jane said nothing. When Ygerna
looked up and asked her another unintelligible
question, Jane nodded and smiled appreciatively.
Over Ygerna's shoulder, Wayne caught Jane's eye
and smiled with amusement.

When Ygerna had finished, she quietly lifted the
pot and carried it outside. She dumped the remaining mud onto the ground and set down the pot to
catch rainwater. Then, catching the drizzle on her
hands, she wiped them off.

Ishihara and Ygerna's husband continued to chop
and split wood rhythmically.

Ygerna called out to her husband, who stopped
swinging his ax and turned to look at her. They
spoke briefly, then he nodded and brought his ax
back to the hut. Leaving it inside the doorway, he
walked back toward his flock of sheep. The dog that
had remained at the hut trotted after him.

"I guess they decided we're okay," said Wayne,
looking out the doorway.

Ygerna walked back inside the hut and knelt by
the fire again.

Ishihara paused and turned to speak to Wayne
and Jane. "I have made a small amount of rudimentary progress communicating with Emrys."

"Is that his name?" Jane asked. "Hers is Ygerna.
That's all I've learned."

"Yes, he is named Emrys. He knows a few Latin words and phrases after all. When I first spoke to him, he kept that a secret, but he has opened up now. His limited Latin facilitated our communication. I now know a few words and phrases in his own language."

"Do you know what he's doing now?" Wayne nodded toward Emrys as he hiked up the slope toward his flock of sheep. "Where's he going?"

"I believe Ygerna told him to bring back a sheep to slaughter for dinner," said Ishihara. "We must wait and see what he does to know if I understood their conversation correctly."

Jane looked up the hill sharply. "Then we've made a change in their lives—a big one. Every one of their sheep must be valuable to them."

"Your apparent status as a lady has made the sacrifice worthwhile, I believe," said Ishihara.

"Hold it," said Wayne. "We can't possibly eat a whole sheep, even the whole bunch of us."

"His family can eat the rest, or sell it," said Jane. "But maybe we should move on tomorrow morning. We could be much too disruptive to this family."

"We still have no money to buy food elsewhere," said Ishihara.

"I don't think we're going to do any real damage," said Wayne. "This kind of thing isn't likely to change history. Come on, Jane—one sheep?"

"We should be careful, at least," said Jane. "As Hunter keeps saying, no one knows where the threshold of change lies. What if some descendants of Emrys and Ygerna are important at some point in English history? Or even on the world stage someday, even centuries later? And what if we disrupt their immediate family in some way that alters their health or survival?"

"You have a point," said Ishihara. "However, if we can return the value of their sacrifice, we lower the likelihood of changing their lives because of the sheep."

"What do you mean?" Wayne asked.

"I will cut as much wood as I can without revealing that I am not human. This will save Emrys from the chore. If we can help in other ways, I suggest we do so."

"Yeah, I get it."

"You were right," said Jane. "Look."

Up on the hill, the dog Emrys had taken with him had cut one sheep out of the flock. Emrys had already started back and the dog was herding the single sheep back down the slope with him. Emrys's son and the other dog had moved behind him and prevented the rest of the flock from following.

A metallic squeak sounded in the hut. Jane turned and saw Ygerna open the small metal door in the chimney over the fire. Using a cloth to protect her hands, Ygerna pulled out a loaf of bread in a pan. She set it down on the hearth and closed the oven door.

When Emrys arrived with the sheep, he took it behind the hut. Jane felt relieved. Butchering sheep would be normal for him, but she did not want to watch. Ishihara continued to cut and split logs.

Jane sat patiently, glad to be out of the drizzle and relieved that they would be fed and, she felt certain, given shelter for the night. On the other hand, the realization that she was trapped with Wayne and Ishihara for at least several more days finally sank in. Even when Hunter arrived, she might not be able to get away immediately. Surviving in this time without money to spend would require genuine effort.

Ygerna kneaded more bread dough and put it in the bread pan. While it rose she went outside and around to the back. Her children trailed after her, but Wayne and Jane stayed inside the hut.

After a few minutes Ygerna came back inside, carrying a large cut of mutton. She knelt again at the hearth and began cutting it into smaller pieces with a large knife. Outside the hut again, she filled a large cookpot with water from a cistern and carried it back to the fire. She hung the pot over the fire and dropped the chunks of mutton into the water. In a few minutes, the water began to boil.

"Smells horrible," Wayne whispered.

"The meat can't be bad," said Jane quietly. "It's really fresh. Maybe mutton always smells like that. I've never had any."

With effort, Emrys carried a large, bulging cloth bag to a tree and threw a rope over a low-hanging branch. From the size of the burden and the blood soaking the bag, Jane saw that it held the sheep carcass. He hoisted the bag into the air, high enough to keep the dogs away from it.

Jane understood that the cool temperature would preserve it for a while. It still looked like too much meat for his family alone to eat before it spoiled. Obviously, he had the same problem every time he slaughtered a sheep, so he would have some normal routine to avoid wasting the meat. She wondered what it would be.

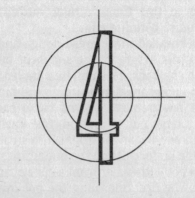

The drizzle continued through the afternoon. As the day cooled, the wind came up and the drizzle turned to rain. Emrys called for his son to bring the flock back to a small pen behind the hut. Then the boy joined the family inside. Ishihara went on chopping wood.

Emrys started to close the door of the hut against the rain. With a questioning glance at Jane, he paused to point to Ishihara.

"Ishihara, come in," Jane said in English. "If you were human, you'd be exhausted by now."

"Of course." Ishihara brought his ax, stopping to wipe the mud from his feet on a patch of grass before he came inside the hut. Then he dried the ax blade on a rag that hung on a hook next to the other ax.

Just as Emrys closed the door, Jane saw that Ishihara had stacked more new firewood than Emrys had cut and split before they arrived.

Once Emrys had closed the door, the fire warmed the hut quickly. Ygerna ladled chunks of boiled mutton onto wooden plates that already held pieces of bread. She took one first to Jane, then served her supposed servants. Emrys received his dinner next, followed by Ygerna and the children.

By now Jane was very hungry. She did not really like the mutton, but she knew that Emrys and Ygerna had sacrificed a sheep for their benefit, so she ate it all. The bread, chewy and dense, tasted better than it looked. After everyone had eaten, Ygerna served some sort of herbal tea in wooden cups.

Jane and Wayne did not speak. However, Ishihara pointed to objects around the hut and asked the children to tell him what they were called. Sometimes Emrys and Ygerna, laughing, helped them.

"Ishihara seems to be learning to speak with them quickly," said Jane. "I guess his knowledge of Latin helps, but I wonder how thoroughly he can pick up their native language."

"He does very well," said Wayne. "He learned rudimentary Chinese quickly because he can apply linguistic principles from the languages he knows to a new language."

"I see." Jane nodded. Since Ishihara had no memory lapses of the kind humans routinely had in the learning process, once he learned patterns and vocabulary, he immediately possessed full use of them.

Ishihara turned to Wayne. "They want to know where we came from. What shall I say?"

"We have to justify our Chinese clothing," said Jane. "That is, we have to explain why it's different. I doubt they ever heard of China."

"Maybe you can just tell them we came by ship across the Channel," said Wayne.

"That's it," said Jane. "Tell them we were shipwrecked by a storm."

"I understand," said Ishihara. "This will explain why we have no belongings or money."

"Yeah," said Wayne. "It's perfect. That's why a lady with servants could be broke."

Ishihara spoke to their hosts, including the children, in short phrases sprinkled with Latin. Ygerna, in particular, asked more questions. Finally she and Emrys both nodded in understanding.

For the night, Jane was given the children's sleeping pallets. The children moved behind the curtain with their parents. Emrys gave Wayne and Ishihara clean wool blankets to roll up in on the floor.

Jane bundled up on the sleeping pallet. The hut remained warm and cozy from the fire. She fell asleep to the sound of rain on the roof.

In the morning, Jane awoke to the sound of the children talking and giggling. Ygerna hustled them outside; when Jane opened her eyes, she saw through the open doorway that the rain had stopped, though gray clouds still covered the sky. Under her blanket, she carefully arranged her robe in its proper position, then got up to find the outhouse.

Outside, Wayne was splashing water on his face at the cistern. Ishihara had already begun to chop wood again. The air was cool and brisk.

When Jane returned to the hut, Ygerna was stirring a pot of hot porridge over the fire. She served wooden bowls of the thick porridge to everyone around the table. Jane called in Ishihara, in order to continue his masquerade as a human.

"Now what do we do?" Wayne asked quietly in English. "Are we going to have to leave now?"

"I don't know," said Jane. "Maybe we shouldn't put too much burden on one family."

"Should I ask?" Ishihara asked.

"We should be careful how we phrase the question," said Jane. "We don't want to insult them."

"They probably assume we want to get on the road to our ultimate destination," said Wayne. "They heard last night that we were shipwrecked and left with nothing, but we still must have been going somewhere."

"Good point," said Jane. "So where are we going? We'd better have our story straight."

Ygerna and Emrys listened curiously, watching them as they all ate.

"I only know the year and our location," said Wayne. "I have no idea what's going on in history now. Where could we have been going? Maybe London?"

"I can't help," said Jane. "This is why Hunter keeps hiring historians to take with him."

"I have some rudimentary history of this time, but no more," said Ishihara. "The Romans settled London several centuries ago under the name Londinium, but it's a long way from here. We can't actually go there if we're going to find MC 6 in this area."

"We better say we were coming to this area all along," said Jane. "That will explain why we won't go very far. But we don't know where we are, do we?"

"On the modern map, yes," said Ishihara. "But I know very little about significant locations in this time."

"Ask Emrys," said Jane.

"What's that going to accomplish?" Wayne snickered. "He already knows we're lost."

"Exactly. And no matter what he says, we'll tell him this is our destination."

"Of course," said Ishihara. He turned to Emrys and spoke briefly in a mixture of Latin and British. Then he switched back to English. "The village on top of the highest hill is Cadbury. The hill itself is called Cadbury Tor. This is the home of a man named Artorius Riothamus."

"Cadbury what?" Wayne asked.

"Tor. It means a high hill in the local language."

"Oh."

"Is MC 6 going to show up there?" Jane asked.

"I believe so," said Wayne. "These component robots have been continually drawn to people of power in the hope, I judge, of influencing them to do less harm to the humans within their power."

"Then Cadbury Tor really is our destination," said Wayne. "Tell him that."

"And add that we cannot pay for lodging because of the shipwreck," Jane added.

Ishihara spoke to Emrys again. The shepherd responded, nodding, and gestured outside. He grinned and gave Ishihara a friendly slap on the shoulder.

"He has complimented my ability to cut firewood," said Ishihara.

Jane smiled, struggling to suppress a laugh.

"Emrys wants to go to Cadbury today to sell the rest of the sheep carcass and some of the extra firewood I have cut. He says he knows that this 'humble hut,' as he calls it, is not good enough for a lady such as Jane, but he has thanked me for the labor I have saved him."

"Do you think we could stay here another night, if necessary?" Wayne asked.

"I think if we expressed interest, and I continue to cut wood for him or find other ways to help him, we would be welcome," said Ishihara.

Jane was relieved to hear that, but said nothing.

"Good," said Wayne. "Tell him we'll be happy to go to Cadbury with him. If we can't find a place to stay there, then we can talk to him about coming back."

"Tell Ygerna that my leg is well, and thank her for the mud poultice," said Jane. "Otherwise, I'll have to fake a limp all day."

Ishihara spoke again to Emrys and Ygerna. After breakfast, Emrys sent his eldest son out again with their dogs to take the flock for the day. Then, at Emrys's direction, Ishihara helped him load firewood and the bagged sheep carcass into the donkey cart.

Jane looked around the countryside in the brisk morning air. Shepherds led their flocks out again in the distance. Smoke rose from the other huts. Life here, at least today, appeared calm and stable.

While Emrys hitched the donkey, Ygerna and the younger children came out to watch with Jane and Wayne. She pointed to the cart and spoke sharply to Emrys.

He nodded and spoke to Ishihara, who began rearranging the wood in the cart.

"What's wrong?" Wayne asked quietly. "What does Ygerna want?"

"She told Emrys we must see that the lady can ride in the cart," said Ishihara. "I will form a seat for her with the wood."

When the cart was ready, Ishihara lifted Jane into the cart. She found her footing on the uneven firewood and sat down. Once she had settled into the seat he had made, she found that it was actually comfortable.

The sheep carcass lay in the front, near her feet. She was glad Emrys had put it in the cloth bag. From her high seat on the cart, she looked down at Wayne and Ishihara.

Ishihara turned to Wayne. "Emrys has room for one more next to him on the driver's bench. I will walk, of course."

Wayne nodded and climbed up next to Emrys.

As Emrys shook the reins to drive the donkey, Jane looked down at Ygerna and the children. The kids waved shyly. She waved back, smiling.

The donkey strained under the load but pulled it forward. The cart creaked slowly out to the road. Ishihara walked near the rear, next to Jane.

When they reached the road, Jane saw that it was soft and muddy from yesterday's drizzle. However, she did not see any tracks in it; the mud had not been stirred up. The donkey's hooves and the wheels of the cart sank into it somewhat, but did not get stuck.

Jane enjoyed the slow, quiet ride. Now that her immediate worries about shelter, food, and safety had been satisfied, she relaxed. She could not plan her escape from Wayne and Ishihara in any detail until she knew that Hunter's team had arrived in this time, and where they were located. For now, she had nothing to do but observe whatever she could for future reference.

Emrys and Wayne could not make casual conversation, so they did not speak; Jane had no desire to talk to Wayne unless she had to. The cart swayed gently as the donkey plodded slowly along. Jane watched Cadbury village as they drew closer.

A wall ringed the village on the plateau. The fact that the village was protected this way, and lay on the flat top of a high tor surrounded by earthwork ramparts at the base of the tor, told her that this area was not always as peaceful as it was today. She remembered that MC 6's specialty in Mojave Center had been social stability, and wondered what had drawn him here.

The journey to the base of the tor took over an hour. By that time, they had passed a couple of people walking along the road. Other people, some of them driving carts or riding horseback, came and went from the tor. As Jane saw the open gate in the earthworks clearly, she looked first at the donkey, then down at Ishihara.

"Is this little donkey going to make it home again? He must be worn out."

"Emrys expects to sell the wood and the meat. The return load will be much lighter."

Sentries at the gate glanced at the cart and waved them through without stopping them, though they stared in wonder at Jane in her Chinese robe. Emrys drove the cart up a steep slope to the top of the tor. Jane saw Wayne looking around with interest and did the same.

The defensive earthworks turned out to be more than a single wall. Four concentric walls ringed the base and the lower portion of the slope. Starting just inside the gate, cobblestones paved the road.

"It's bigger than it looked from outside," said Jane, as the donkey began pulling the cart up the steep angle. "Ishihara, how big is this place?"

Ishihara scanned the area briefly. "I cannot see the far side of the tor, but if the shape of its base as a whole is roughly a circle, I estimate that outer wall encloses approximately seven hectares."

Up ahead, the road led through an open, nearly square gatehouse in the high wall that surrounded the summit and the village within it. Sentries held spears lazily on the top of the wall, talking among themselves. Jane thought the wall had been constructed of wood until the cart passed through it. Then she found that only a breastwork of wood faced the outside; the bulk of the wall was made of unmortared stone.

Inside the wall, they found themselves in a bustling village. Jane turned and looked up at the inside of the wall. Now she could see that the sentries stood on top of a wooden platform that ringed the top of the stone wall, with the wooden breastwork rising high enough to protect them from attackers who might have crossed the first four earthen ramparts on the lower slope. All around the village, the interior side of the wall was designed the same way.

"It looked so modest from a distance," said Jane. "This is pretty impressive."

"I estimate the perimeter of this wall to be over three-quarters of a kilometer," said Ishihara. "Since the wall has neither straight sides nor represents a circle, my approximation is quite rough."

On the far side of the main gate, a two-story hall built of timbers rose over the rest of the village. Emrys turned the cart down a narrow side street, but Jane continued to look at the hall. If MC 6, after returning to his full size, was going to seek the seat of power, he would probably find it inside that hall.

Jane saw that Wayne also had taken a second glance at the hall. He almost certainly had reached the same conclusion, but she said nothing. Maybe something else was on his mind. In any case, MC 6 was still microscopic, possibly somewhere on the ground at their feet this very moment.

Emrys drew up the cart and greeted a couple of men behind a booth. Chunks of meat lay out on a wooden counter, with flies buzzing over them. The men called out heartily and waved for him to step down.

As he did so, Jane realized that the men at the booth and most of the other villagers nearby were all staring at her. Then she saw that they looked just as curiously at Wayne and Ishihara, in their more modest Chinese peasant clothes. None of the villagers spoke, however.

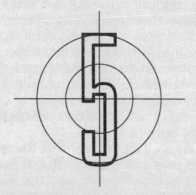

Jane watched in silence as Emrys drew the cloth bag back from the sheep carcass. The other men examined the meat as Emrys talked, and then they unloaded the carcass and carried it to their booth. One of them carefully counted a few coins into Emrys's hand. He slapped the other man on the shoulder with a quick smile and mounted the cart again.

"It's interesting to watch," Jane said to Ishihara. "In all the times and places we've visited, dickering over small business transactions seems to be about the same."

"Yes," said Ishihara.

Emrys shook the reins. This time he drove the donkey around a corner and followed the narrow, crooked streets to the main doors of the large hall. He spoke briefly to a sentry, who slipped inside.

"I wonder who lives here," Jane said casually to Ishihara. She did not want to express too much interest in the building, for fear of alerting Ishihara and Wayne to her belief that MC 6 would eventually come here. Even if they had reached the same conclusion, she could pretend she had not. "I guess Emrys knows they burn a lot of wood in a building this size."

"I expect so." Ishihara changed languages and spoke to Emrys, who answered at some length.

Wayne turned in the seat to look at Ishihara. "What did he say?"

"Emrys says this is the palace of Artorius Riothamus," said Ishihara.

"Artorius is a Latin name," said Wayne. "Is he a Roman warlord who stayed behind or something?"

" 'Riothamus' seems to mean 'High King,' " said Ishihara. "He is also called Artorius the 'Dux Bellorum.' "

"That's Latin for 'War Leader,' " said Wayne. "But what does it mean as a title?"

"I presume that not every High King leads his men out to war personally," said Ishihara. "However, that is merely my own surmise."

"We're roboticists, not historians," said Jane. "Ishihara, do you have any history at all that pertains to this time and place?"

"Very little," said Ishihara. "However, I believe that Artorius the High King may be the man upon whom the legend of King Arthur is based."

Wayne scowled. "This place doesn't look much like the Camelot I learned about as a kid."

"The legend was built by storytellers and poets and novelists over many centuries," said Jane.

A tall, burly man dressed in a worn leather tunic came outside with the sentry and several other men. The tall man spoke to Emrys briefly, then nodded. The other men started to approach the cart but stopped, looking at Jane.

"Emrys has sold the entire cartload of wood," said

Ishihara, raising his arms to lift Jane. "I will help you down."

Jane stood up and let Ishihara move her to the ground. As the workmen began carrying armloads of wood into the palace, the first man counted out a handful of coins into Emrys's palm. Emrys opened a leather pouch at his belt and slipped the coins inside.

Jane remained with Ishihara, looking around the village. People filled the narrow streets in every direction. She saw booths and shops offering food, clothing, pottery, and leather goods for sale.

When the wood had been unloaded, Emrys spoke to Ishihara and waved for Jane and him to get into the cart. Ishihara lifted Jane back into the empty cart, then climbed in after her. Emrys started the donkey again.

"He is going to buy us clothes," said Ishihara. "He says he will do this as his appreciation for my help."

"Thank him again for his hospitality," Jane suggested. "We were trying to pay him back, after all."

"I did," said Ishihara. "I think he may also be embarrassed by our clothes. He will be happier once we blend in with everyone else."

First Emrys took them to a shop that sold used women's clothes. Jane found that all the gowns were made of wool. She chose a simple brown one. In a stall in the rear, she changed out of her outer Chinese robe, but kept the underrobe that Hunter had provided to make the Chinese robe more comfortable. It protected her from the scratchy wool of her new gown.

Emrys dickered with the shopkeeper and paid for the gown. Jane carried her Chinese robe and trousers out over her arm. Then Emrys drove the cart to another shop that sold only men's tunics.

Jane stood patiently by the cart as Wayne and Ishihara tried on tunics and leggings. This would have been an ideal moment to escape them, if she had anywhere to go. However, Wayne and Ishihara knew as well as she did that Hunter had not arrived yet.

After Emrys paid for the new tunics, he drove to another street where food was for sale at each stall. He bought a bag of flour and a small earthenware jar of sea salt. Then he treated his guests to a midday meal of mutton stew and fresh buns.

Jane decided that Ishihara's help had not made a big difference in Emrys's life. Although they had certainly changed his life today, she felt he was simply taking a normal day in the village. He was probably doing what he would have whenever he had come into the village next.

Jane decided to take her Chinese robe back to the hut and give it to Ygerna as a gift. If Ygerna did not want to wear it, she might be able to use the material to sew something else. Women here did not seem to wear trousers, but Jane felt that Ygerna could use the material to make something useful for herself or for her children.

After they had finished eating, they all mounted the cart again. Emrys drove them out of the village, back down the cobbled road to the base of the tor. Jane leaned against the back of the cart and gazed at the peaceful countryside. This time, Ishihara rode in the front of the cart behind the front seat. No one spoke until the cart had passed through the main gate of the outer earthwork. Then Emrys spoke over his shoulder to Ishihara.

Emrys and Ishihara conversed for several moments.

"What is it?" Wayne asked. "Are we going somewhere else today?"

Jane sat up, straining to hear.

"No," said Ishihara. "We are returning to his hut. However, he remembers that in years past, the palace of Artorius requires the most wood when soldiers are gathering here in the spring. They must be fed and kept warm at night."

"What soldiers?" Wayne asked.

"He says that every spring, soldiers from all over the land of the Britons come here from their winter homes. During the winter, only Artorius's personal troop lives here. Then, as spring progresses, Artorius will gather his army and lead it against the Saxons."

"So is Emrys one of these soldiers?" Wayne asked. "Is he going to report in?"

"No," said Ishihara. "He says that if the palace needs so much wood now, they will need meat, too. Instead of waiting until the soldiers arrive, he wants to drive some of his flock back here tomorrow and sell the sheep ahead of his fellow shepherds. The others are still waiting to hear that the men have moved back to the palace."

"That one building can't hold a whole army," said Wayne. "How many are coming?"

"That is unclear," said Ishihara. "However, the seven hectares of the enclosed tor offer a wide expanse of open land below the walled village. I expect his soldiers sleep out there."

"Yeah, that makes sense."

Jane did not move or speak, but she felt her heart beating faster with excitement. Wayne expected MC

6 to return to full size tomorrow, and that mean Hunter would probably reach the same conclusion. If Hunter's team arrived tomorrow, then Wayne and Ishihara would want to ride back to the village with Emrys. If they took her, she could look for an opportunity to escape them, or at least to alert Hunter to her whereabouts. If they left her in the hut, she would simply leave after they had gone. She only had to hope that Wayne would not order Ishihara to stay at the hut with her.

Wayne said nothing more.

Jane wondered if Hunter would think that Ishihara's labor at Emrys's woodpile was going to create too great a change in the lives of Emrys and his family. The coins he had received today, and the food, were not too extravagant. If he got the jump on the other shepherds, however, he might become substantially more wealthy than he would have been if Ishihara had not cut all the extra firewood.

At first, she could not reach any conclusion about it. Ishihara did not seem disturbed by the problem. Then she realized that Emrys still could sell only the wood and sheep he already owned. Maybe he would only benefit modestly from Ishihara's help.

Jane smiled to herself. Tomorrow she would look for Hunter at the tor.

Steve felt himself tumble gently on his back to damp, soft ground. Overhead, low, gray clouds covered the sky. In the west, a diffuse glow revealed the setting sun behind the clouds.

He pushed himself up to a sitting position. The land nearby combined rolling hills with occasional stands of trees. On some distant hills, he saw flocks of sheep with shepherds and dogs.

"You are both unharmed?" Hunter looked at them as he stood up.

"I'm fine," said Steve.

"Yes, of course," said Harriet cheerfully. "Mm, smell that rich earth. Springtime in England. It's so green and fertile here."

Hunter helped her to her feet. "I will begin calling Ishihara at intervals. I do not expect him to respond, even if he is here, but I must attempt to reach him."

"Why wouldn't he answer you?" Harriet asked.

"Wayne will almost certainly instruct him either to shut off his reception or to listen but not answer. Whatever plan Wayne has in mind will rely on evading us."

"I don't see a castle," said Steve, suddenly alarmed. "Are we in the wrong place?"

"No." Harriet pointed to a large hill not too far in the distance. Large earthen ramparts ringed its base. A small walled town sat on its summit. "In the medieval sense, no castle ever stood at Cadbury. The modern term, Cadbury Castle, refers to the entire walled tor and its village. While we remain in this time, we might call it Cadbury Tor, instead."

"So that's where we're going?"

"Yes," said Hunter. "It is farther than it looks. We must begin."

"Okay." Steve hoisted the cloth bag over his shoulder. "Lead the way."

Hunter led them across the open grassland toward a narrow dirt track that wound toward the tor. As they walked, Steve looked up at the tor again. Some people rode horseback, drove wagons, or plodded out

of the main gate. He supposed they were on their way
home to other villages or huts in the countryside.
Others walked or rode into the tor from outside,
including two men in steel caps holding spears as
they rode.

"Is that what a Roman fortress here looked like?"
Steve asked. "It resembles the temporary camps we
saw the Roman legions build in Germany, but this
one looks permanent. I thought the Romans would
build something more impressive than this."

"This is a post-Roman construction," said Harriet.
"The village on the plateau is fortified in part
by unmortared stone, including Roman masonry
brought from elsewhere. The gatehouse has touches
of Roman architecture, too. But the overall design
is Celtic."

"You mean now that the Romans don't rule here
anymore, the Britons are doing everything their
way again?"

"In practical matters, Britons never forgot their
own traditions," said Harriet. "Further, funding was
an issue. Roman administrators at the height of
their power could pay many men to quarry, move,
and cut stone, and hire others to build with it.
Post-Roman Briton rulers had to make do with
ramparts of rammed earth."

Steve nodded.

She pointed to a similar hill much farther in the
distance to the north. "That's Glastonbury Tor. It
still exists in our own time, as well."

"So with the Romans gone, the Britons are back
where they started in fighting the Saxons?" Steve
asked. "Except for what you said about Roman cavalry tactics?"

"Not completely. The Britons still have some

advantages from their Roman cultural experience, including roads, cities, and towns. However, hordes of Saxons have already settled along the eastern coast."

"You said this Artorius, who uses Roman cavalry tactics, is the historical basis for King Arthur. Back in Room F-12, we agreed to pretend we wanted to sell horses to him. So he rules here? Or what?"

"Artorius is a charismatic cavalry captain with some Roman-style training. He has become Riothamus, or High King, of the Britons by leading the Celtic fight for their homeland against the Saxons."

"If the Saxons landed on the eastern coast, along the English Channel, why is he here?" Steve asked. "If we're in what's central southern England in our own time, then we're a long way from the Channel."

"That's right," said Harriet. "You see, the Saxons have been coming for many decades. They have conquered and settled considerable territory on the eastern side of Britain."

"All right, I get it. Now the Britons are fighting the Saxons along some boundary that runs through the middle of the country."

"Yes. Of course, the boundary is jagged and uneven, usually represented by rivers or ridges. And because of constant fighting, it is in flux throughout these years. Artorius had to establish his base far enough behind the border to have a wide buffer zone."

Steve nodded. "Since the Saxons are on foot, it would take them a lot longer to march all the way here than it would take his cavalry to ride out to meet them."

"Correct."

"Hunter, I have to ask you the question that comes up in every mission," said Steve. "We know that MC 6 will return to full size around here somewhere, but exactly what's he going to do? Where should we look for him?"

"That is usually Jane's area of expertise, of course," said Hunter. "Without a roboticist to call upon, I will have to make a judgment. Based on my experience in how Jane has made her earlier appraisals, I expect that MC 6 will want to stop the war between the Britons and the Saxons that causes so much suffering."

"Yeah, that sounds like what she'd say," said Steve. "We found MC 3 and MC 4 trying to stop wars, too. Of course, we prevented that."

"We must prevent MC 6 from doing it, as well," said Hunter. "According to the history I took from the city library, Artorius held the Saxons at bay during his lifetime but they eventually overwhelmed his successors. If MC 6 succeeds in working out a long-term settlement, however, the England of medieval, Renaissance, and ultimately modern times will never develop, deeply changing the course of history."

"Oh, piddle." Harriet laughed lightly. "That possibility is preposterous."

"It is?" Steve looked at her in surprise. Her bluntness startled him. "Why?"

"You see, the Saxons, Angles, and Jutes invaded Britain because of tremendous population pressure on the Continent north of the Roman Empire and their displacement by the movement of more powerful tribes, such as the Franks and the Goths."

"Why did they come to Britain in particular?" Steve asked. "Couldn't changes in what happens here cause them to go somewhere else?"

"As a matter of fact, they moved into Gaul in this era, as well, to settle on the Loire," said Harriet. "But by comparison, Britain was lightly populated at the time. The desperation of the Saxons to migrate and the comparatively modest numbers of the Britons to protect their island dictated this period of British history. No agreement among individuals could stop these forces."

"That makes sense to me," said Steve. He liked the logic of this argument. It fit the fact that the team's appearance in the past on other missions had not, to their knowledge, disrupted their own time.

"I have already acknowledged that I cannot measure the degree to which chaos theory can be applied to history," said Hunter. "And I accept this history as accurate. However, the First Law requires me to consider the danger of changing history, no matter how remote it may be. After all, as a robot, MC 6 can expect a much longer life than any human, barring injury. If we do not take him away soon enough, he can remain in this time to continue working out compromises as new hostilities develop. Of course, in any case we have to take him before he reaches the time he left and explodes with nuclear force."

"You're the boss, as I said earlier," said Harriet. "I'm just doing my duty as your historian in reporting my opinions to you."

"As far as our search is concerned, the First Law would still impel MC 6 to attempt an end to war, no matter how hopeless his long-term chances are," said Hunter. "Following the judgment that Jane made about earlier component robots, I believe this imperative would take him to Artorius or maybe even the Saxon leaders."

"I have no argument with that," said Harriet. "You would know more about robots."

"I also feel that the creation of Arthurian legend will almost certainly change if the history upon which the earliest chroniclers based it no longer occurs in the same way. This is possible even if the historical events do not change. The legend seems to be quite important in British culture and its branches in the United States and other parts of the former British Empire."

"Now, *that* I agree with," Harriet said emphatically. "Arthurian legend—of course it could change if historical events alter. That legend has had great cultural influence over the centuries and must not be allowed to change."

"I wouldn't want to lose it, either," said Steve. "I followed it as a kid—the stories of Camelot and the Knights of the Round Table, and Lancelot and Guinevere."

"Of course, we will not find them here," said Hunter. "They are legend, not history."

"So we agree with you about not letting MC 6 change history after all," said Harriet. "We will find him."

"I guess if Ishihara had responded to your call, you'd have told us by now," said Steve.

"That is correct," said Hunter. "I have heard nothing."

By the time they reached the main gate at the base of the tor, torches burned in brackets over it. Sentries in leather jerkins and leggings picked up their spears and began to swing the solid wooden doors closed. They waited, however, as Hunter strode up to them.

Steve, remembering that no Britons here had seen anyone of Chinese descent, hung back in the shadows with his head down.

"We seek shelter, friends," Hunter called out cheerfully in British. "You have lodging in the village, do you not?"

"We have inns here," said one of the sentries. "What is your business?"

"I breed horses in Gaul," said Hunter. "I seek new land in which to breed my horses. Even in Gaul, we have heard of the great cavalry leader Artorius. I would speak with him and ask if he will accept some of my finest stock."

"Yes? Where are your horses? Still in Gaul?" The sentry grinned. Next to him, his companion laughed.

"We took ship from Gaul with five horses, but rough seas cast them overboard."

"Yes?" The sentry eyed Hunter cautiously.

"Have you crossed the Channel, friend?" Hunter asked. "At this time of year?"

"No," said the sentry. "Rough, is it?"

"The same rains that fall here in the spring can rage over the seas even harder," said Hunter.

The sentry nodded, looking over Hunter's tunic. Then he glanced at Harriet and Steve. "We are far inland here. How did you come?"

"We landed on the southern coast at Devon, then followed the roads here."

"How did you know which way to come?"

"Every shepherd and villager on the way knows how to find Artorius."

The sentry nodded again.

"Who are your companions?"

"My wife and our servant, a man from the farthest side of the Roman Empire."

"Very well. Welcome, friends." He stood aside for them to enter.

Steve still kept his head down as he followed Harriet through the gate. In the darkness, broken only by flickering torchlight over their heads, he knew the sentries could not see him clearly. In any case, they did not bother to look; they were closing the gates behind him.

Hunter led them up a long, cobbled road to the village at the top of the tor. The sentries at the main gate of the wall also watched them approach by torchlight. When Hunter stopped in front of the gate, Steve lowered his head again and remained back in the shadows.

"We seek lodging," said Hunter. "The sentries below passed us."

"I thought as much," said the man in front of him. "Are you the last in for the night? If so, we'll close this gate behind you."

"Yes, we are the last."

"Come in, then." He, too, stood aside.

Hunter led Harriet and Steve through the gate into the village.

The streets of the village were lit by torches over a few of the doors. People still walked through the streets, especially outside taverns. The mood seemed peaceful.

"It's not like the peasant villages in medieval China, is it?" Steve asked. "Those were just homes for farmers. This is more like a small town."

"I see shops, stables, and taverns," said Hunter, looking up the length of the streets in each direction. "Only the taverns are still open for business, however. This is a village in a civilized society. It also has nothing in common with the villages we saw in ancient Germany, which belonged to a primarily hunting and gathering society."

"Roman Britain was something of an outpost in the Roman Empire," said Harriet. "However, London, York, and Bath were established as Roman bases—modest by the standards of the Mediterranean, but civilized urban areas in comparison to the earlier British Celtic villages. Cadbury Tor has evolved from an older country village to something of a town, obviously because of Artorius bringing power and wealth to the area."

"Jane could be here," said Steve. "Wouldn't Ishihara want to get Wayne and Jane some good shelter like this?"

"Yes," said Hunter. "For tonight, however, we must do the same. Our search can begin tomorrow."

"Lead the way," said Steve.

Hunter approached a quiet tavern. Inside, several men sat at tables drinking. Some wore leather jerkins and leggings similar to those of the sentries. Others wore woolen tunics like Hunter's and Steve's. A short, gaunt innkeeper limped forward to look up at Hunter.

"Yes, friend?"

"We seek lodging for the night," said Hunter. "For my wife and me and our servant."

"Show me your money."

"How much do you want for the rooms?"

"That will depend on whose money you carry."

"Roman coins from Gaul." Hunter opened the pouch at his belt and spilled some coins into one hand. He held out his palm so the other man could see them. "Mostly copper. Some silver. No gold."

"No gold, eh?" The innkeeper scowled at the money. "Five silvers."

"For one room?" Hunter shook his head. "Two coppers, friend."

"Four silvers, then."

Hunter closed his fist around the coins. "We have traveled far. Two coppers is a fair price."

"Find it elsewhere, then, if you can."

"Very well." Hunter turned abruptly and strode toward the door.

Steve and Harriet moved outside ahead of him. Just as they got outside, however, the innkeeper hustled after them. At the sound of his footsteps, they turned.

"Four coppers," called the innkeeper. "For our

friends from across the Channel. A special price."

Steve grinned. "I showed Hunter how to bargain on earlier missions," he whispered to Harriet.

"Three coppers," said Hunter.

"For a room with two feather beds," Harriet whispered. "On the ground floor, with a fireplace."

"I have no such room with a fireplace of its own," said the innkeeper, glancing at her.

"Two coppers, then," said Hunter.

"Three coppers for a room with two beds and a bar on the door," said the innkeeper. "On the ground floor near the back door to the latrine."

"Very well," said Hunter. He dropped three copper coins into the man's open palm.

"Welcome, friends. Come inside." The innkeeper stepped aside and swung his arm toward the door.

Hunter accepted. Harriet and Steve followed him back inside. Some of the men drinking at the tables glanced up again, but without much interest.

The innkeeper picked up a stub of candle on a small dish and led them down a narrow hallway. He opened the door to a small room and swung it back. Then he stepped out again.

Steve glanced around. The two beds nearly filled the room, leaving only a small space between them. A long, narrow shelf ran along the wall from the doorway. This room was intended for sleeping, no more.

"It is acceptable," said Hunter. "In the morning, I expect bowls of water for washing."

"As you wish. Sleep well, friends." The innkeeper handed him the candle dish and left.

Steve drew back the covers to one bed. "Well, it looks clean enough." He pushed on the pallet. "Straw, not feathers. It'll be scratchy."

Harriet laughed lightly. "I trust we'll survive the night somehow."

"I will spend the night by the door, on guard," said Hunter. "Do you need anything outside the room before I bar it for the night?"

"Yeah," said Steve, with a grin. "A quick trip out to the latrine. And don't bar it before I get back, either."

"Of course I will not." Hunter sounded puzzled.

"That was a joke, Hunter."

When Steve returned, Hunter barred the door and touched the candlewick lightly with one finger to put it out. As the humans got into bed, he listened for any sounds suggesting danger and heard none. He remained alert throughout the night, motionless to conserve his energy.

Morning arrived without incident. When Hunter heard footsteps elsewhere in the inn, he went out and repeated his request for bowls of water from the innkeeper for Harriet and Steve. By the time the innkeeper fetched water from the cistern and Hunter returned to the room, both Harriet and Steve were up and dressed.

Soon they went to the dining area in the front. Steve brought the team's bag with him, since they had not paid for a second night in the room. The men from the night before were not there, but two other men in woolen tunics sat hunched over bowls of hot cereal. The fire in the fireplace had gone out.

"Remember to speak British," Hunter whispered in that language. "We will be overheard and we want to sound as though we belong."

"As you wish." Harriet drew in a deep breath. "Ah, feel that brisk spring air again. I love it."

"I'm hungry," said Steve, moving to an empty table. "This one okay?"

"Of course," said Hunter.

The innkeeper hurried out to greet them and offered breakfast. In the daylight, he took a second glance at Steve in surprise, but said nothing. For breakfast, he served wooden bowls of hot oatmeal and herbal tea. He also brought out a small dish of honey for flavoring.

"It's quite familiar," said Harriet, inhaling the steam rising from the oatmeal. "I suppose oatmeal and honey haven't changed a great deal over the years."

"It's good," said Steve. "Not that I like oatmeal much. Good enough, though."

"I reviewed my conversation with the sentries at the outer gate," said Hunter. "While my claim to be a horse breeder and trader got us inside the tor, I now believe that Steve is correct that this will not bring us to an audience with Artorius. Without horses to show a prospective buyer, the pose will no longer be useful."

"At least we're inside." Steve shrugged. "Maybe we can just hang around here in the village and ask for people of Jane's and MC 6's descriptions."

"I prefer to act more aggressively," said Hunter. "Harriet, we discussed some other possible social roles before we left. Would you suggest another?"

"Well, you didn't want to be soldiers because that might be more dangerous to Steve," said Harriet. "But without other supplies to bring Artorius— food, armor, or weapons, mainly—that's the best way to get the attention of a military commander. You could start by joining up and then look for an opportunity to meet him."

"Hold it." Steve swallowed and put down his spoon. "I have another problem with this. I learned the hard way in the Caribbean that I'm no fighter."

"Really?" Harriet turned to him. "What happened, may I ask?"

"I tried fighting a couple of times." Grinning, Steve shook his head. "One guy almost carved me up with a rapier, but someone interrupted us. Running around on deck during a boarding was even crazier. And what kind of soldier can Hunter be? He's not allowed to harm humans."

"Our goal does not require fighting," said Hunter. "We simply want to be involved in life around Artorius, where MC 6 will probably appear. Harriet, how soon will Artorius go to war again?"

"That's hard to say," she said slowly. "In a sense, despite short-term truces and treaties, Britain is more or less in a state of ongoing war between Britons and Saxons."

"Can you make any sort of calculated estimate about when the next campaign will begin?" Hunter asked.

"Let me think out loud for a moment. The earliest chronicles don't give the years in which battles took place, let alone months and days. The odds are, however, that none ever took place here at Artorius's capital, or that fact would have been mentioned."

"If he has to march somewhere else for battle, we'll have plenty of warning," said Steve.

"Most of the battle sites were vague," said Harriet. "Some are completely unknown, but Artorius will certainly have to go out on campaign to reach them."

"Hunter." Steve switched to English and spoke in a whisper. "For this subject, we can't risk being understood by anyone else. If Artorius goes out on campaign while we're here, are you going to let us desert from his cavalry to avoid getting into a battle?"

"We must always remember that MC 6 is our first goal, but of course I cannot put either of you into more danger than necessary under the First Law."

"I think you just dodged my question." Steve grinned wryly. "Can we desert or not?"

"If necessary, I will certainly take you out of danger," said Hunter.

"That hasn't always worked out as we've planned," said Steve. "But I'll go along with this if you really want to."

"I suggest we also expand on our personal story." Harriet whispered in English also.

"What do you have in mind?" Hunter asked.

"We should maintain our claim to have traveled from Gaul recently, or we will be branded liars. But in order to explain your desire to fight for Artorius, we should explain that we are Britons."

"And we just moved to Gaul for a while to live?" Steve asked skeptically. "That sounds a little thin to me."

"That's not all," said Harriet. "I suggest we come from Linnuis, a British district which the Saxons have taken over. This would explain why we were displaced in years past and fled to Gaul when a ship was available. Now we have managed to come back to Britain."

"I understand," said Hunter. "This improves our story. Where is Linnuis?"

"Historians believe Linnuis was modern Lincolnshire. It lies on the coast of the North Sea, northeast of here across the width of Britain."

"We will use this as our story," said Hunter, speaking British again. "How should we make our attempt to enlist with Artorius?"

"After breakfast, I suggest you ask the sentries at the main gate to the village."

"Very well," said Hunter.

"I can hardly believe this." Steve laughed lightly, still whispering in English. "We rode dinosaurs, sailed with buccaneers, and ambushed Roman legions. We landed in the middle of World War II, met Marco Polo and Kublai Khan, and now we're going to join King Arthur. Wow."

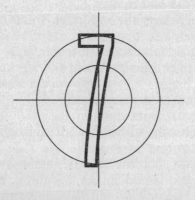

After breakfast, Steve followed Hunter and Harriet out of the inn to the street. Merchants had already opened their shops and stalls by now. The village gate stood open and people walked up and down the streets.

Steve liked the idea of accompanying Artorius and his men for a while, as long as no battles with Saxons were involved. He wished Jane could see him join up; she would probably find it funny and she might even be impressed by it. Then his mood dampened as he wondered where she was.

"Hunter," Steve said, falling into step with him just before they reached the village gate. "How about spreading the word around the village that we're looking for Jane before we sign up?"

"I can do that," said Harriet. "While you two enlist, I will spend the day asking about Jane around the village. And I will ask about our missing friend."

"Will you be safe here?" Hunter asked.

"Yes, I think so."

"The village is peaceful," the sentry said. "She will be safe."

"All right," said Hunter.

"Here. I'll carry the bag today. You'll need your hands free."

"Thanks." Steve handed it to her.

"Of course." Harriet turned and strolled up the street.

Steve shrugged, disappointed.

Different sentries stood by the gate. As Hunter approached, one turned toward him, leaning on his spear.

"Good morning, friend," said Hunter.

"Fair," said the sentry.

"My friend and I had to flee our home in Linnuis to escape the Saxons. We would like to fight with Artorius. How do we volunteer?"

"You want to volunteer?" The sentry eyed Steve with curiosity for a moment, saying nothing. Then he turned back to Hunter. "All right, then. Step over here."

The sentry moved to the middle of the open gateway and pointed. On the steep slope of the tor below, Steve could see forty or fifty armed men milling around. Some were mounted; others walked horses by their reins. From this vantage point, he could also see a pen holding a few other horses on the far side of a storage building.

"Lucius takes the new recruits out every morning," said the sentry. "They just finished breakfast a short time ago. Go down and ask for Lucius."

"Thank you," said Hunter. "If those are the new recruits, where are the others?"

"Most of the veterans have not arrived from their winter homes. Artorius's personal troop is at leisure today, except for those on patrol."

"I see."

Steve and Hunter walked out of the gate and down the cobbled road. The new recruits were slowly mounting and lining up, with several burly men in leather jerkins shouting orders. One man on a large bay waited silently, watching them all. Hunter walked up to him.

"Are you Lucius? We are Hunter and Steve."

"Yes. What do you want?" Lucius studied Hunter with interest.

"We wish to volunteer and ride with Artorius against the Saxons."

"Hmm. We can always use a man of your stature, if we have a horse to carry your weight." Lucius glanced at Steve. "Do you speak our language?"

"Yes, I speak British."

"From where do you come?"

"From the eastern side of the Roman Empire. We have been in Gaul until recently."

"Gaul?"

"My wife and I fled Linnuis ahead of the Saxons," said Hunter. "The three of us arrived here last night."

"Well, you are no Saxons. Do you ride? Have you fought before?"

"We both can ride," said Hunter. "However, we have not fought much."

"Do you have horses?"

"No."

Lucius frowned. "I feared so. We are always short of good horses."

"You are taking new recruits," said Hunter. "Will you take us or not?"

"The personal troop of Artorius has its full complement of three hundred," Lucius said sternly. "But word has gone out for last year's veterans to come from their farms and villages. Most of them will have their own mounts and a few may bring new ones, too." He pointed to the wooden building on the slope behind the new recruits. "I will see if you can ride or not. Go to the tack building and tell the groom to mount you."

"We have no weapons," said Hunter.

"The armorer's store stands on the near side of the building," said Lucius. "Stop there first and tell him to outfit you. And hurry; we will ride out soon."

Steve followed Hunter through the crowd of men and horses. Ahead, Steve saw the armorer standing outside a wooden building watching them come. He was a short man with long, gray hair and beard. When he turned and moved inside the building, he walked with a pronounced limp.

By the time Steve and Hunter reached the building, the armorer had come outside again. He tossed two round wooden shields on the ground in front of them and then dropped two short swords on the shields. Without a word, he limped back into the building.

"I guess he knew what we wanted when he saw us coming," said Steve, picking up a sword and shield. "No swordbelts or scabbards, though."

"Roman short swords," said Hunter. "British shields. I suppose the armor will be made of leather."

"So it is," said the armorer gruffly as he came out again. He leaned two spears against the wall of the building. "But not for you, friend. You're too big. I'll have to boil a new hide and slap it on you when you ride back this afternoon."

"Boil it?" Steve asked.

The armorer snickered, revealing broken teeth. "A first-timer, eh? Well, you'll learn." He reached inside the door and pulled out a large, rigid piece of leather, about the size and shape of Steve's torso. It bent at the shoulders, with a hole for his head; the bottom was cut short at the waist. Thongs dangled from holes along each side. "Lace those on."

Steve slipped it over his head and onto his chest and abdomen. "It's hard."

"Boiled leather will turn a blade almost as well as steel," said the armorer. "It just wears out faster, over time. But if you had the money to buy steel, you'd be wearing it."

Hunter moved to Steve's side and began lacing the leather armor on him.

"How do you get the shape?" Steve asked.

"I boil it in a vat of water till it's nice and soft. Then I slap on your body steaming hot, and you'd better be wearing a tunic when I do." The armorer grinned. "It takes the shape of your body and cools that way."

"I see. Uh, what happened to the guy this belonged to before?"

"He died of a fever." The armorer stepped back inside again and came out with two conical caps. "Here." He tossed a cap to each of them.

Steve put on the cap. A leather band inside the rim padded it somewhat. It fit him well enough.

A boy of about ten led two horses up to them, already saddled and bridled.

"The groom saw you coming," he said shyly to Hunter. "We got you the biggest horse we have."

"Thank you." Hunter took the reins and mounted. "He will be fine."

Steve slipped his shield on his left arm and carefully stuck a sword through the belt of his tunic. Then he mounted the second horse, which pranced and shook. He kept control of his mount, however. The armorer handed him his spear.

"He's a good horse," said the boy. "But he spent all winter in pasture. He's only three and he hasn't had a rider since last fall."

"I like him," said Steve. "Hunter, the troop is riding out. We'd better go."

"Yes." Hunter reached down to take his spear from the armorer. "Thank you, friends."

Steve and Hunter rode back across the slope and followed the rear of the troop out the main gate at the base of the tor. The morning air was still cool, but the clouds overhead had begun to scatter. Steve grinned with excitement, wondering what Lucius would have the troop do.

They did not ride far. In the open, rolling country outside Cadbury, Lucius ordered the troop to split into squads, ordering each to fall out and drill separately. Because the squads formed immediately, Steve saw that they had already been assigned.

Hunter and Steve rode up to Lucius, who had reined up on the crest of a hill to observe the troop.

"We are ready, friend," Hunter said heartily. "Where should we go?"

"Eh? Oh, yes." Lucius pointed to a nearby squad. "These are squads of ten, but that one is short. Your squad leader, Cynric, will drill you."

Steve followed Hunter to the squad. A short, stocky man had been shouting orders to the group. Just as Steve and Hunter reached them, Cynric raised his spear and turned his horse. He led the squad away in a canter.

Steve kicked his own mount and followed. His young horse eagerly took off. Hunter's mount also moved into a canter, more reluctantly. Steve left him behind as the squad rode across the open grassland.

Soon Cynric took the squad into a full gallop. Then, without warning, he pulled up sharply. Just as the squad gathered around him, he kicked his mount again and took off in another direction. Steve laughed and followed with everyone else.

This time, Cynric led the squad in a long, sweeping curve back toward their starting point. Three of the riders took the curve too fast and lost it, angling wide; two others tried to take it too sharply and lost speed. Steve watched Cynric's movements carefully and followed him without trouble, with two other riders. Hunter remained behind him.

Cynric stopped again on the slope near Lucius. Steve reined up behind him, and Hunter joined him a moment later. They waited for the stragglers to canter back to them.

Steve, getting a good look at the others' faces for the first time, saw that most of them were teenagers. He supposed they had either come from villages or shepherd families. They would know how to ride casually, but not on military maneuvers.

Cynric studied Steve and Hunter with pale blue eyes. "Who are you, anyway?" His voice was gruff.

"I am Hunter. This is my friend Steve."

"And Lucius sent you to me."

"Yes," said Hunter.

"Well . . . I don't get a lot of grown men in this troop. You two ride better than most of these youngsters. Can you fight?"

"We have never fought on horseback," said Hunter.

"I'm not surprised," Cynric said sourly. He threw his spear into the ground and raised his voice to the entire squad. "Form a line and follow me. You will ride at full gallop past this spot and throw your spears into the ground next to mine—if you can."

Jane rode in the back of Emrys's cart again that morning. As before, Ishihara sat in the front and firewood filled the rest of the bed; Wayne rode on the seat with Emrys. However, this time they followed almost half of Emrys's flock of sheep. One of his dogs herded the sheep forward along the road toward Cadbury Tor.

When Jane saw the riders leaving the main gate of Cadbury Tor, she looked up. Even at a considerable distance, she was sure that the large rider trailing the rear of the troop had to be Hunter. The fact that a man Steve's size rode just ahead of him seemed to clinch it.

Jane glanced up at Wayne and Ishihara. Wayne yawned and watched the sheep. Ishihara was rearranging the firewood slightly.

"Ishihara," said Jane. She did not know what she was going to say, but she wanted to distract him from seeing Hunter and Steve. Wayne was not as likely to recognize them, even if he looked in their direction.

"Yes?"

"Uh, how safe are we?" A concern about the First Law would command a robot's attention the most.

"What do you mean?" Ishihara looked at her.

"Well . . . we're very vulnerable, don't you think?"

Jane frantically tried to think of a specific worry she could express to him.

"To what?"

"To the unknown. I mean, we hardly know what's going on around us, do we?"

"Thanks to Emrys and Ygerna, we have food, clothing, and shelter. Neither they nor anyone in the village seem to have any pressing fears."

"It's not as civilized as China was." Jane glanced at the troop again. They had ridden away from the tor, but Hunter remained easily recognizable at the rear.

"We are much safer here than in Roman Germany," said Ishihara.

"Yeah . . . that's true, I guess. But maybe a war will start here, too."

"Perhaps. I expect to have some warning, however. We all knew that a battle would begin outside Moscow in 1941, but we survived."

"It's a terrible risk under the First Law, isn't it?" Jane stretched, and gazed casually around in several directions to camouflage another look toward the troop. Now the column of riders had divided into small groups. For a moment, she could not find Hunter. Then she saw that his group had begun to ride away, fast. She relaxed a little.

"The searches for MC 3 and MC 4 ended in much greater danger than we face here so far," said Ishihara. "I assure you again that I will take you and Wayne away from danger if necessary." He patted the spot on his torso in which he had placed the belt unit.

"I know," Jane said quietly. She looked at Wayne. He did not seem to have noticed Hunter and Steve.

Jane wondered if the troop would ride back into

the tor while Emrys was still selling sheep and firewood there. If so, she might have a chance to get Hunter's attention. She would have to hope that Wayne and Ishihara would not notice Hunter first.

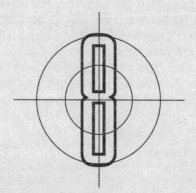

Steve moved into the line as the squad prepared to throw spears. Ahead of him, the other riders waited for Cynric to wave his arm in a sharp downward slash. Then the first rider kicked his mount, rode at full gallop about fifty meters, and threw his spear into the ground next to Cynric's.

When Steve's turn came, he hefted his spear in his right hand and looked at Cynric. At the signal, he took off and eyed his target. Several other spears had stuck in the ground near it; others had fallen flat. Steve threw his without slowing his mount.

His spear flew forward but instead of sticking in the ground, it landed flat on the grass. He reined in near the other riders and turned. Hunter came next.

At the signal, Hunter rode forward. As he neared the target, he threw his spear. It angled through the air and stabbed into the ground next to Cynric's.

Around them, scattered all over the rolling hills, the other squads conducted similar exercises.

As Hunter rode up next to Steve, Cynric nodded approval. When the squad had finished throwing their spears, they gathered around Cynric. Steve suddenly wondered if he might be cut from the troop and Hunter retained.

Cynric said nothing about it, however. "Leave your spears where they are. Form two lines facing each other, two horse lengths apart. When I signal, move against the rider across from you. I want to see you handle your swords and shields. Lay on hard, now—this is no game."

As the riders formed the lines, Steve and Hunter moved across from each other. At Cynric's signal, all the riders rode forward. Steve found that the real challenge to this exercise was holding the reins in his left hand while using the shield on his left arm to protect himself.

Hunter's blows were light, at least by Hunter's standards, and always landed on Steve's shield, no matter how he moved it. Steve swung his own sword with more abandon, secure in the knowledge that Hunter could easily block each stroke with his own shield. On each side of them, the other squad members did the same.

Cynric rode slowly behind each line, circling the squad. He shouted instructions and encouragement at times. After a while, he ordered them to halt.

Steve lowered his sword and shield and grinned at Hunter with relief.

"Take up your spears again," Cynric called out. Then, as the riders moved out of their line, he turned to Hunter. "You sit a horse well for a man your size."

"Thank you for the kind words." Hunter nodded acknowledgment. "Tell me something. I always heard that the Saxons have no horses. In Linnuis, I never saw a mounted Saxon. Why do you have us perform this exercise against another man on horseback?"

"A man who fights for Artorius must be at home on his mount," Cynric said sternly. "Besides, occasionally a Saxon patrol will take a horse or two. But you are right. In the main, a battle against the Saxons means a small British cavalry against a much larger army of Saxon foot."

Steve had to dismount to pick up his spear. While he was on the ground he handed a couple of the other spears up to other squad members. Then, clumsily cradling his own in the crook of his left arm, he managed to mount again.

Hunter plucked his own spear from its vertical position in the ground and rode up next to Steve.

"Harriet radioed me a moment ago," Hunter said quietly. "She is well, but has seen no sign of MC 6."

"Is she just going to walk up and down the streets of the village all day?"

"Perhaps not. She has seen some from the citadel come out to shop. Since Artorius probably lives there, she hopes to speak to them."

"Hey, maybe she can get inside somehow."

"Follow me!" Cynric shouted suddenly, holding spear high. "Now!" He rode away abruptly, as before.

The squad, caught by surprise, took off after him.

The remainder of the morning continued the same way. Cynric ordered specific exercises with weapons, often divided by sudden orders to charge across the hills. These charges sometimes were straight, and sometimes curved; the riders had to stop and wheel around quickly, changing direction. Finally, at midday, wagons came out of the tor to bring bread, cold mutton, and water to the squads. The horses were watered and rested.

In the afternoon, the nature of the exercises changed. Now the squads worked together, maneuvering in combinations of ten, with a hundred riders each. Steve stayed close to Hunter. Finally, in late afternoon, Lucius gave the order to return to the tor.

As Steve and Hunter rode on weary mounts with the rest of the troop back to the main gate, Cynric rode up alongside them.

"You will join us in the camp," said Cynric.

"You are in a camp?" Hunter asked. "I have not seen a camp. Where is it?"

Cynric grinned. "Behind the village, on the far slope. The green recruits are kept out of the way."

Steve wondered what Hunter wanted to do about Harriet, but he did not ask. A blunt conversation would have to wait until they were out of the hearing of others. He looked up at the village and wondered if Jane was there somewhere.

Hunter knew that he could not call Harriet. He had no idea if she had company within the hearing of her lapel pin. If they could not find her in the streets of the village, then he would have to wait for her to call him again.

At the paddock, each rider unsaddled and brushed down his own mount. Then they were dismissed. Hunter, however, walked back to the armorer, who had a fresh leather boiling in a big vat.

"Is that for me?" Hunter asked.

"Keep your tunic on to protect yourself from the heat," the armorer said gruffly.

Steve stood by as the armorer pulled the steaming leather out with a long, hooked pole. The leather had a hole already cut out of the middle and the armor lowered it over Hunter's head. Moving quickly, the armorer tied it snugly around Hunter's waist with a piece of old rope. Steam rose from the leather.

"I'm glad he already had one my size," Steve muttered. "That's hot."

"No one ever died of this," growled the armorer. "I've been doing it for years. That tunic he's wearing will protect him."

"I am fine," said Hunter.

The armorer quickly tied the leather around Hunter's arms, as well, so that it fit tightly around his entire torso. Then he began to punch holes up and down the sides in straight lines, ignoring the uneven shape of the leather. By the time he had finished, the leather no longer steamed.

The armorer knocked on the leather against Hunter's chest. It gave slightly. "Still soft," he muttered. "Just wear that for a few more minutes."

Hunter nodded.

The armorer drew a knife and began trimming the leather. He cut it off at Hunter's waist and straightened the edges running down the robot's sides from under his arms. By the time the armorer had cut the last pieces off, he had to use a great deal of effort to slice the blade through the leather.

"Should be finished now." The armorer knocked on the Hunter's back. This time, it made a thunking sound. "That's it. Here, I'll lift it off."

Hunter bent forward so the armorer could raise it over his head.

Steve saw that the leather had now solidifed into a hard shell that maintained its shape, just like the leather he was still wearing.

"It needs a little more trimming. And some of these holes need to be punched out more cleanly. I'll do that. When you come back in the morning, I'll have thongs for you to lace the sides closed. After that, you keep it."

"Thank you."

The armorer nodded and carried the new armor inside his building.

Some recruits walked around the slope to the rear side, avoiding the village. Others took the cobbled road up to the village gate. Hunter and Steve walked back up to the gate together.

"Hunter, Harriet here." Her call came through his internal receiver.

"Yes, Harriet."

"I can see you walking back up the hill and I got a moment alone. Did you see MC 6 anywhere?"

"No. Tell me where you are. We must confer."

"I think we'd better talk now. I'm in the palace. And if I leave, I don't know if I'll be welcome back."

"What do you mean?"

"Well, I struck up a conversation with some of the women who live here. One is the wife of an adviser to Artorius and another is the grown daughter of some elderly military man. I'm not sure exactly what he does. But I explained that my husband and our servant had come from Linnuis by way of Gaul to fight and that I was now unescorted."

"They simply invited you into the palace?"

"Not exactly. We talked for a while. They are very conscious of social class. I am clearly not a peasant. When they asked about you, I explained that you were a very wealthy and successful horse breeder and trader. They know that Artorius needs an ongoing supply of good horses."

"What happened?"

"Gwenhwyvaer, the daughter of the military man, has been very kind. We get along well. She invited me to stay with her. But she had to argue with some of the others. I don't want to seem ungrateful by asking to go out again today. But if everything is still okay tomorrow, maybe I can meet you in the village."

"Then you have safe lodging for the night?"

"Oh, yes. As long as I don't offend anyone. And I may have a chance to spot MC 6 here, if he has regained his full size by now."

"Very well. I will wait for you to call me again. If you feel any potential danger, call immediately."

"All right, Hunter. Harriet out."

Hunter related the conversation to Steve. "Instead of going up to the village to look for her, I suggest we go to the camp in the rear to find out where we will sleep."

"Good idea."

Jane had hoped to remain in the village until the troop returned. However, Emrys's business did not take long enough. In the morning, he had bargained with men from the palace for the sheep. After some spirited haggling, Emrys had sold them all to the palace, improving the deal by offering the firewood, as well. He had received both coin and barter in the form of some wool and two piglets that had to be tied inside the wagon.

At Jane's request, Emrys had agreed to spend more time in the village. They visited an open-air stall at midday to eat and then browsed through the shops. However, in the middle of the afternoon, he had decided to return home. As they had taken the wagon back down the slope toward the gate in the outer wall, Jane had seen the troop of riders still maneuvering in the distance.

Jane watched Wayne and Ishihara carefully all day. In turn, they looked at everyone in the village, but only glanced casually at the troops on maneuver in the distance. She could not figure out why Ishihara did not examine the troops more closely.

Although she did not want Ishihara to notice Hunter if he had not seen him already, she wanted to find out what priorities he was using. She waited until the wagon had left the main gate and traveled down the road, leaving the troops out of sight around a bend. Then she raised the subject indirectly, speaking in English so that Emrys would not understand.

"Ishihara."

"Yes."

"As I understand it, Wayne will only instruct you to let me go if he can either get MC 6 or bargain for him with Hunter. Right?"

"Yeah?" In the front seat by Emrys, Wayne turned around and glared at her suspiciously. "We've already established that. What of it?"

"When are we going to get this underway? I don't want to live here forever."

"Calm down, will you?" Wayne said sourly. "I don't like waiting, either. But we can't do anything till we find at least one of them."

"So we're just going to visit the village every day and look around? What if Emrys doesn't want to go back tomorrow? He has chores at home."

"If we have to, we'll hike in ourselves," said Wayne. "Right, Ishihara?"

"If you wish."

"And then we just stand around?"

"Do you have a better idea?"

Jane looked at Ishihara. "Tell me if you know where MC 6 or Hunter is."

Ishihara turned to look at Wayne. "What should I do? You instructed me not to discuss this subject with her or in front of her."

Wayne grinned. "Go ahead and answer."

"I do not know where MC 6 is," said Ishihara. "I may know where Hunter is but I am not certain."

"Nice try." Wayne snickered. "You can't order him to tell you something he doesn't know."

"That's not the point," said Jane. For the moment, she decided not to sound too eager to learn what Ishihara might know about Hunter. "Do you guys have a plan or not?"

"I've calculated that MC 6 will return to his full size in the tor," said Wayne. "I've instructed Ishihara to prioritize spotting him."

Jane decided to risk reminding them of the troops. "Does that include people outside the tor? Say, shepherds like Emrys, or traders coming to and from the tor?"

"I have looked at the people we have passed on the road," said Ishihara.

"How about those riders?" Wayne asked. "The guys with the spears? They were too far for me to see clearly."

"None of them is small enough to be MC 6," said Ishihara. "One of them is large enough to be Hunter. With the movements of the riders, I was not able to ascertain this for certain, even at the maximum magnification of my vision. A man the size and build of Steve rode very close to him."

Jane said nothing. She had recognized Hunter. At least she now knew what Ishihara had seen. The reason he had not mentioned it in her hearing before was that Wayne had instructed him not to do so.

"You're sure that MC 6 is not riding with that outfit?" Wayne asked.

"Yes."

"Good. For now, we'll let Hunter waste his time with them. We'll focus on finding MC 6 first."

Jane said nothing more.

Steve and Hunter found the camp on the far slope. A single large command tent stood at the top. Two unhitched wagons stood next to it, full of closed wooden crates. Small campfire sites, cold at the moment, dotted the area, surrounded by small bundles of furs and cloth bags.

Cynric met them there and showed them which campfire belonged to their squad. He also pulled some old blankets out of a crate in one wagon and gave them to Steve and Hunter. The other squad members had not come back yet.

After Cynric walked away, Steve sighed and looked up at Hunter.

"What is wrong?" Hunter asked. He set his blanket down on the ground.

"We'll be sleeping out under the stars. It was cold last night. Even next to the fire, we'll be cold."

"I noted the temperature last night. It should not be harmful to you."

"No . . . but it'll be uncomfortable." Steve grinned. "Don't worry about it. I just hope it doesn't rain."

"I suggest we walk up to the village. The sun will not go down right away. Maybe we can buy some additional bedclothes for you."

"Okay." Steve glanced up. The sky had more clouds than before, but he did not smell rain.

They walked back up to the village and strolled through the streets. Hunter found a stall selling furs and bargained down the price on a coverlet of rabbit pelts stitched together. Steve slung it over his shoulder gratefully.

Hunter noted when the other green recruits in the village left again. He and Steve followed them back to the camp, where the campfires now burned. Some men passed bread to each squad; pots of mutton already boiled over the fires. A brisk breeze blew across the twilit countryside.

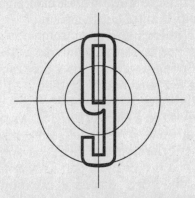

As Steve and Hunter sat down around their campfire, Cynric finally introduced each squad member by name. In the gathering darkness, he directed one of the men to ladle mutton out of the pot into wooden bowls already filled with chunks of bread.

"Cynric," said a young man named Cai. "What will we do tomorrow? More of the same?"

"More of the same." Cynric looked around the group sternly. "You have much to learn before you can keep an angry Saxon from killing you."

"Will it be different when the veterans arrive?" Cai asked. "Will we ride with them?"

"Our troop will remain together," said Cynric. "Lucius will lead us. When the veterans first begin to gather, they will not bother to ride, except on their own. Once the bulk of them have arrived, we will practice maneuvers with them."

"When will we go out on campaign?" A taller young man named Cadoc looked up from his bowl.

"No one can be sure," said Cynric. "It depends on what word Artorius hears from scouts and returning veterans. He won't plan a campaign until he knows something about the enemy."

None of them spoke.

"You can be sure we're going somewhere," Cynric added. "Spring always brings a new campaign for Artorius. You need not doubt that."

The other men nodded.

Cai chewed on a piece of bread for a moment and glanced at Steve. "I've never seen a man of your appearance before, yet you speak our language well. How did you two come to join us here today?"

"It's a long story," Steve said cautiously. He was not sure how much detail Cai wanted.

"We met in Gaul," said Hunter casually. "My wife and I hail from Linnuis, but we fled the Saxons on board ship across the Channel."

"I have known men from Gaul," said Cadoc. "None looked liked you, Steve."

"I come from the eastern end of the Roman Empire," said Steve. He glanced at Hunter, who watched him silently. Steve decided he was free to improvise. "I traveled to Gaul as a servant to another horse breeder. We met Hunter and I began working for him, instead."

"But where is this land you come from?" Cai asked. "My grandfather served all over the empire and told me stories about his travels. Do you come from Egypt? Judea? The Parthian border?"

Steve looked at Hunter again.

"His family comes from farther east than that," said Hunter. "From Sina, the land of silk."

"Never heard of it," said Cynric. "Not that I care." He looked into the distance, where the sun had gone down. A faint glow over the horizon still lit the sky. "Well, men, shall we take our nightly stroll through the village?"

"You walk through the village every night?" Hunter asked. "Why?"

Cynric grinned. "For a goblet of mead, maybe. Or to meet a woman in a tavern. Maybe just for a walk. It keeps these young farmers and shepherds in the saddle during the day, when they know they have a visit in the village at night."

Steve caught Hunter's eye. "We'll join you."

"Hunter, you can see your wife."

"Perhaps," said Hunter. "First, we have business in the village. A certain friend of ours may live in the village now. We will look for him."

"As you wish." Cynric shrugged.

As the squad walked back up to the village, Steve noticed that the other squads were doing the same. Not everyone went, however; a few others stayed around their fires. Some of the men had already stretched out in their bedrolls.

The streets of the village had only a few people, just as the night before. Cynric sought out the most crowded tavern, though, calling out to friends he found there.

Hunter and Steve bought mead in dented metal goblets and stood among talkative, laughing men in the middle of the crowd. Steve saw that Hunter was looking around, so he did not bother; Hunter's height advantage and better vision meant that he could do the job better and faster, anyway.

Steve found the mead interesting at first, but not really to his liking. He held the goblet and glanced back out the open doorway. A small group of other men sauntered past.

Hunter continued looking around the crowd.

Steve slipped away from him through the crowd, moving toward the door. The noise in the tavern covered his footsteps. With a glance over his shoulder at Hunter's back, he set his goblet down on a small table and stepped back outside. He hurried down the street.

After the five earlier missions, Steve no longer worried about changing history through ordinary actions. He did not believe that he would alter the fate of Britain or the shape of Arthurian legend by getting away from Hunter for a few minutes to explore the taverns on his own. At the same time, he knew he would feel more free to act spontaneously without Hunter.

Steve followed the men in front of him into another tavern. This place had about half the crowd of the last one, but the patrons here were also cheerful and talkative. Steve moved to the bar and ordered more mead. When he turned, he found almost every man in the place looking at him.

Slowly the tavern grew quiet.

Steve looked from face to face. For the first time, he realized that Hunter's company had protected him. No matter how curious or hostile the Britons had felt, none had confronted him in front of Hunter. The squad members had asked their questions politely. Now he was on his own.

A young man with shoulder-length, reddish-blond hair smirked at him over a goblet.

Steve decided to take the initiative. "Good evening," he said pleasantly.

"So it is, stranger." The other man snickered. "Who are you, then? Some Pict from the wilds up north?"

"Ha!" Another man sneered. "I say he's a a wild man from across the western sea."

"I came from Gaul," said Steve, forcing a smile.

"You're no Gaul," said the first man. "But you speak our language. What's your name, then?"

"Steve."

"Eh? What kind of name is that?"

"Well, it's short for Steven," Steve said lamely. "What's your name?"

"I heard of a Stephen who followed Jesus," said another man, quietly.

"What's your name?" Steve asked the blond man again, still trying to sound cheerful.

The man ignored his question. "You were named for this Stephen?"

"It was the origin of my name," Steve said hesitantly. He had been named after a relative in the immediate sense. More importantly, he realized that the men around him really wanted to know something about him. He would have to speak up to satisfy them.

"You are a follower of the Church, then." The blond man cocked his head to one side, studying Steve's face.

"Yes." Steve did not know if Britain in this time had different denominations or sects, so he said nothing more. He also could not tell exactly what opinion the others might hold about this.

"What is your purpose here?"

"My friend and I have joined the troop of new recruits," said Steve.

"That's true," a man called from the back. "I saw him riding back through the gate with a big, tall fellow."

The blond man smiled, finally. "I am Bedwyr. I lead a scouting patrol."

"Really? Do you live here year-round?" Steve felt a wave of relief at his friendlier tone.

Bedwyr slapped him on the shoulder. "Forgive our questions, friend. Artorius will lead us all out on campaign soon, but we are getting restless."

Steve glanced around. Not all of the other men had accepted his presence; some still eyed him suspiciously. However, no one else spoke.

"Something wrong, friend?"

"I've only seen a few taverns in your village. How about showing me around a little?"

Bedwyr laughed. "Why, sure." He threw back his head and emptied his goblet. "Come on, let's go."

Steve took another swig of his mead and set his goblet down. As he followed Bedwyr out of the tavern, he was glad to see that no one else joined them. He did not feel that he had been made welcome, exactly, but being treated with indifference was good enough.

Bedwyr started up the street, pointing to another small building with flickering candles in the window. "That's a good place for food," he said. "Not so much for drinking."

"Tell me something," said Steve, falling into step next to him. "You're the only one who seemed to think my joining Artorius meant something. The others still aren't so friendly. What's different about you?"

"You mean, regarding you?" Bedwyr shrugged. "I spoke up first because I was the most curious about you. And Artorius needs every good man he can get."

"So I have heard."

"The Saxons don't ride, but they come across the Channel like endless packs of wolves. Any man who will face them is all right with me. But you must understand that in these times, not everyone loves a stranger."

"Yes, I do."

"Enough of that." Bedwyr pointed up in the moonlight toward the palace as they walked. "My barracks lie there, in the citadel. You can't see it well in the darkness, but all of Artorius's personal troop lives with him in that quarter. We are sworn to die for him if necessary."

"Are you in his personal bodyguard?"

"No," said Bedwyr. "You misunderstand. He has a personal household troop of about three hundred, depending on casualties from time to time. We live here permanently and accompany him on every trip he takes. His bodyguards are a special group of only twenty."

Steve wanted to get inside the palace somehow to look for MC 6. However, he did not want to appear too eager for fear of making Bedwyr suspicious of his motives. He decided to approach the subject obliquely.

"How does a new man join the personal troop?" Steve asked. "To maintain the number around three hundred, men killed in battle obviously must be replaced."

"A man's loyalty must be proven. For instance, my father died fighting in Artorius's personal troop when I was young. My mother sent me when I came of age."

"So connections are important."

"Yes, or special courage and sacrifice on the battlefield." Bedwyr nodded.

"What about working in the palace?" Steve asked. "Artorius must have people who keep the fires burning and cook the food and clean up."

"What of it? You came to fight."

"Not for me," said Steve. "I'm looking for a friend. A little guy. He's coming here, but I don't know if he's already arrived or not. He wasn't in Lucius's troop, so I wonder if he's working in the palace."

"Ah. I understand now." Bedwyr shrugged. "People like that, the servants . . . I pay no attention."

"Who would know? Someone in the palace who hires the servants, I guess."

"Yes."

Steve waited, hoping Bedwyr would offer to help. When he did not, Steve decided to ask him outright. Steve only hoped he would not offend the warrior in some unpredictable way.

"Could you introduce me to this person? I would like to ask about my friend."

"Mm, well, how about another drink, Steve? Even this little village has more taverns than we've seen yet."

"You can't take a stranger to the palace?"

Bedwyr grinned. "You really want to find this fellow. Does he owe you money?"

"No, no." Steve laughed. "But you're right—finding him is very important to me."

"I'll talk to a friend," said Bedwyr slowly. "But no promises. Come on."

"Where are we going?"

"We'll see who's on sentry duty this watch. I know all those guys."

Steve grinned in the darkness. This was progress, at least. In Bedwyr's company, he couldn't call Hunter directly, but he switched on his lapel pin so that Hunter could overhear him.

"How far is it to the palace?" Steve asked.

Bedwyr laughed. "In this village? You've seen it.

Nothing is more than a few minutes' walk."

Steve knew Hunter would get the message from that exchange. They walked in silence through the streets. When they turned a corner, they left the taverns behind.

A single torch burned in a holder over the main entrance to the palace. Two bored sentries sat on stools, cradling their spears. They looked up with interest when they heard footsteps approaching.

"It's Bedwyr," he called out. "And a new friend. Good evening, Aetius. Wake up, Drustan."

They both grinned. "What are you doing here, Bedwyr? The taverns are still open."

"My friend Steve, here, now rides under Lucius. He seeks a friend who may be in the palace."

Drustan frowned. "He can't go inside at this hour. In the morning, maybe."

"I don't need to go inside," said Steve. "My friend is called MC 6."

"Strange name," said Bedwyr.

"He may have taken another on his travels. Maybe I could describe him to you. He's a little guy, slender and about so high." Steve held his hand at MC 6's height. "He probably doesn't talk much, but he's very agreeable. If you tell him to do something, he just does it. And he never hurts anybody—he won't fight, but he'll try to stop a fight between other people. Have you seen him?"

The sentries looked at each other.

"Well, there's little Patricius," said Drustan. "He's only twelve."

"I'm looking for a grown man," said Steve. "Just a little one."

"Medraut's not too big," said Aetius. "But he's no stranger. He's Artorius's nephew."

"One of the cooks caught him scrapping with another young rascal yesterday," said Drustan. "Medraut picks fights all the time."

"You sure he's that little?" Aetius asked. "Maybe he's gotten his growth since you saw him last."

"Well . . . it was only a few months ago."

"I fear we haven't seen anyone like that," said Drustan. "We would notice, I think. But maybe he works in the village somewhere."

"Maybe so. Thank you." Steve sighed. Hunter had certainly heard the entire exchange. MC 6 probably had not returned to full size yet. "Bedwyr, shall we visit another tavern? I'll buy."

"Not so fast," said Drustan, grinning. "Artorius has been coming out for a quick walk every evening. He may come out any minute."

"You mean I could meet him?"

"If he walks out in the same mood as usual, he'll have no objection. He likes to mix with the men this time of year, as the campaign season approaches."

"I think I'll hang around." Steve laughed. "You mind, Bedwyr?"

"Not at all. I'll linger with you. It can't hurt to have a good word with the man at the top."

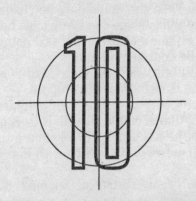

Back in the hut, Jane helped Ygerna prepare another pot of mutton stew. At first, Ygerna had tried to dissuade her guest, but Jane had simply laughed lightly and picked up a knife to cut meat. Ygerna baked more bread and carefully seasoned the new stew with the sea salt Emrys had brought from the village.

Ishihara had gone outside to cut more firewood in the twilight. Emrys stacked the pieces. Wayne alternately paced outside restlessly and sat on a stool inside the hut. The children, now growing accustomed to their visitors, paid less attention to them.

As she cut chunks of mutton, Jane tried to decide how to proceed. Now that she knew Hunter and Steve had joined the troop of riders, she could try to get their attention. On the other hand, Wayne and Ishihara surely knew she hoped to do that. When they went to the village tomorrow, she expected Ishihara would become even more attentive to her than usual to prevent her from escaping. Her greatest fear was that Wayne would leave her here with

Ishihara. Then she would have no chance.

Wayne and Ishihara came inside the hut, followed by Emrys. Jane glanced up but said nothing. Emrys closed the door behind him.

"Shall I tell Jane?" Ishihara asked Wayne.

"Might as well." Wayne shrugged.

"I have spoken with Emrys about tomorrow," said Ishihara. "Based on the number of ewes pregnant in his flock, he has decided to take more sheep to the village tomorrow. We will go with him to look for MC 6."

"Okay." Jane shrugged, feigning indifference. Actually, she was deeply relieved. Apparently they were going to take her; that meant she might have a chance to get away.

When the main doors of the palace opened, Steve tensed with excitement. Six men came out, wearing now-familiar plain wool tunics and leather boots and leggings; a servant inside closed the doors again. Both sentries stood up alertly.

The man in front smiled at the sentries. "Good evening, men. Did I wake you?"

Drustan and Aetius both laughed and shook their heads, their admiration for him evident in their faces.

"No, sir, Riothamus," said Drustan. "Not us."

"Well, I know this is boring duty. I did my turns on watch when I was young."

Steve tried to get a good look at Artorius Riothamus in the flickering torchlight. He seemed to be in his early thirties, of average height and a medium build. His shoulder-length hair was light brown, as was the narrow, neatly clipped beard along his jawline.

"Good evening, sir," said Bedwyr politely. He, too, looked fascinated.

"Good evening to you." Artorius looked at him in the uneven torchlight. "Ah, Bedwyr, isn't it? You lead one of the scouting patrols."

"That's right, sir."

Artorius looked at Steve. "I don't believe I know you, friend."

"I, uh—"

"This is Steve, a man from the eastern end of the Roman Empire," said Bedwyr. "He and a friend from Linnuis have joined Lucius's troop."

"Ah! I'm glad to hear it. Welcome, Steve."

"Thank you," Steve said shyly.

"Have you and your friend ridden before? Can you sit a horse?"

"Yes, sir."

"Good." Artorius laughed lightly and gave Steve a pat on the shoulder as he passed. "We need you." He and his entourage walked on down the street.

Steve turned to watch him go. Artorius was personable and unpretentious, but he also came across as reserved, confident, and supportive of his men. Steve liked him and realized that this personal magnetism, combined with his military successes, helped create the legend that grew after his death.

"Still ready for another drink?" Bedwyr asked him cheerfully.

"Sure."

Harriet had accepted the invitation of Gwenhyvaer, the young woman she had befriended, to her small room. She had recognized the name as the original Welsh from which the more modern

"Guinevere" had been derived. Now a fire burned brightly in a stone fireplace; candles lit the corners of the room. The two women sat on each side of the stone hearth, with fur lap-robes keeping their legs warm.

Gwenhyvaer was stitching the hem of a gown by the firelight. Watching her, Harriet decided that Gwenhyvaer was even younger than Harriet had first thought. Most likely, she was still in her late teens, which made her an adult in this culture.

"How many children do you have?" Gwenhwyvaer asked, glancing up from her sewing.

"Uh—none." Because she and Hunter had not discussed that question, she was caught unprepared.

"No?" Gwenhwyvaer's eyes widened in surprise.

Harriet shrugged, suppressing a smile. "No."

"Oh, my. Did they . . . I mean, did they die young? Or you never had any?"

"I never had any."

"That's so sad. How does your husband feel about this? Doesn't he want sons?"

"We no longer worry about it," said Harriet. "It's all right."

"I hope I have children who grow up." Gwenhyvaer smiled shyly. "My father says Artorius likes me. He's hoping to arrange for us to be married."

Harriet smiled at her youthful embarrassment. "You must love him."

She giggled. "Every woman I know does, I think. At least, the younger ones."

"Has your father been with Artorius long?"

"Oh, yes. He's been advising him on Roman cavalry tactics. My father is part Roman. He served in the legions in Gaul until about ten years ago. So did his father, before the legions left Britain. He was stationed up by Hadrian's Wall, on the Pictish border."

"I see. You come from a long line of soldiers."

Gwenhwyvaer nodded soberly. "The men will be going on campaign soon. My grandfather died in a battle. I wish my father would stay home."

"He still rides with Artorius, then?"

"Yes." She sighed. "But of course he needs my father. The Saxons keep coming and coming. Father says Artorius must ride out and fight them on their land, not wait for them to march here."

Harriet stifled a yawn and glanced at the sleep pallet that servants had prepared for her. With the fire nearby, and using the fur lap-robe as a coverlet, she would be warm here tonight. For now, however, she would stay up talking as late as her hostess wished.

Looking at Gwenhwyvaer, Harriet thought to herself that this teenager could not possibly ever imagine the kind of role she would play in Arthurian legend, fictional though it would become—or across how many centuries she would be remembered, at least in some form.

Jane found the morning routine at the hut the same as the day before. Everyone at the hut ate breakfast and Emrys picked out which sheep he would drive to the village. The only difference, as Emrys drove the cart behind the small flock again, was that he did not take any more firewood. Jane guessed that his family had no more wood to spare. Without the need to load the cart, they left earlier than they had yesterday.

On the way, Jane watched the main gate of the tor ahead, to see the troop of riders again. This time, however, the riders did not leave before Emrys brought his small flock and the cart up to the gate. As they started up the steep, cobbled road to the village, Jane saw the riders gather around some sort of storage building and the paddock, saddling their horses and leading them toward the gate. She could not see Hunter and Steve in the crowd, so she assumed they were inside the building.

"I want to ask Emrys to stop," Ishihara said suddenly to Wayne. "Do I have your permission?"

"Of course," said Wayne.

Jane tensed.

Steve stood behind Hunter just inside the tack building, waiting in line to pick up their saddles and bridles. They had just finished a bland but plentiful breakfast of hot cereal; Hunter identified wheat and barley in it. Then they had walked down the slope, where Hunter had picked up his leather armor from the armorer and laced it on.

Steve's arms and shoulders were sore from the unaccustomed exercise the previous day.

"Hunter, by the time this is over, I'll be in great shape." He grinned and moved up with the line. "Do you think we should stay with the troop even though MC 6 isn't in it?" He lowered his voice. "Maybe we could try for duty in the village, to be nearer the palace."

Hunter turned, looking over Steve's head out the open door behind them.

"What is it?"

"Silence, please," Hunter said quietly.

Steve waited patiently, though other men continued to talk around them. Horses snorted and their hooves clopped outside. Steve guessed that Hunter was attempting to sort out some other sound, but he had no idea what it could be.

"Come outside with me," said Hunter. He left the line and moved back toward the door. The men behind him made room for him and Steve followed closely.

"What is it?" Steve asked quietly.

"I heard the footstep pattern of Wayne Nystrom nearby."

"Yeah?" Suddenly excited, Steve hurried out the door after him. "Jane must be close."

Hunter stopped abruptly. Steve did, too, when he saw Wayne simply walking right up to them with a smirk. He seemed to be alone.

"Where's Jane?" Steve demanded.

"Don't worry. You know Ishihara can't allow any harm to come to her."

"Yeah? He's not here to protect *you*." Angrily, Steve took a step toward him. Before he took a second step, however, he felt Hunter take his upper arm from behind and hold him firmly in place.

"Stop," Hunter added calmly.

"Where is she?" Steve demanded again.

"Why have you approached us?" Hunter asked. "Do you have something to say?"

"I certainly do." Wayne grinned. "Let's negotiate a little."

"On what basis?"

"I've been here a week. That's given me time to start a routine here, to get settled. And to make a few friends. I'm not desperate here, as I was in Roman Germany."

"You say you've been here a week," said Steve. "Does that mean you sent Jane and Ishihara somewhere else?"

"No comment," said Wayne, snickering. "But I remind you that Ishihara follows my instructions. I intend to hold Jane hostage in return for MC 6, if you should find him before I do. And he must be untouched and unexamined."

"I understand your terms," said Hunter.

"You can't just accept that," Steve said hotly, looking up at him.

"I cannot endanger Jane," said Hunter. "You know that, of course."

"I'll give you some time to think about it," said Wayne. "But I warn you not to follow me to find anyone. If we have to jump through time to get away from you, I may not make an offer like this again."

"Acknowledged," said Hunter.

Wayne, still smiling triumphantly, turned and hurried away through the crowd of men and horses.

"Grab him," said Steve, pulling against Hunter's
unbreakable grip. "We can hold him as a hostage for
Jane. You can call Ishihara and tell him. Ishihara
can't let either of them come to harm, so he'd have
to give in."

"I do not dare," said Hunter. "I have no indication
of where they are. Wayne may have left them in
another time or in a place out of range of my signal.
He may have left Ishihara with standing instructions or First Law interpretations that would cloud
the First Law imperative to release Jane. Making an
attempt could simply anger Wayne and cause him
to withdraw his offer."

"Well, what's wrong with that?"

"Maintaining negotiations will provide Wayne
with an incentive to stay in contact with us. If
Jane is nearby, we may eventually be able to track
him back to her, or at least surmise her general
vicinity."

"Well . . ." Steve tried to think of another objection, but could not. "How about calling Ishihara
anyway, and trying to get him to release her?"

"Have you forgotten? I have continued to call Ishihara at intervals ever since we arrived. He has not responded."

"Oh, yeah. But we could just follow Wayne now and find out whatever we can."

"I dare not. Besides, the troop is about to go out on maneuvers, remember?"

"We don't have to stay."

"Leaving so soon will complicate our ongoing presence here. We must maintain our place in the troop for now." Hunter turned, drawing Steve with him. "We must get our saddles and bridles. Again, we will be among the last to ride out."

"Yeah, all right." Steve joined him at the end of the line again. "So you think Ishihara has Jane in some other time?"

Hunter released his arm. "That is not my first estimate. I acknowledge the possibility because it prevents me from acting too rashly, but I doubt the likelihood. Ishihara would probably insist on remaining in the company of both humans to protect them."

"He wasn't with Wayne right now," said Steve. "And in the past, you've been willing to take a chance on one of your educated guesses."

"I wish to prioritize caution at the moment. I believe Ishihara and Jane are probably fairly close. They may be in the village or out in the countryside, but I could not hear or see any sign of them. If we bide our time, I may pick up some clue to their location. Then we can act more aggressively."

"But you're still just guessing."

"I am making a calculation of the odds."

"Uh, right."

Hunter said nothing for a moment. When he spoke again, he lowered his voice. "Harriet just called to say she is well. She remains with the women in the palace."

"Good. That's something in our favor."

They picked up their saddles and bridles and carried them out to their mounts.

Jane sat in the back of the cart up in the village, near the palace doors. Emrys haggled over the sheep with the same man as the day before. From here inside the walls, she could not see the slope or exactly where Wayne had gone, but she could guess. Ishihara and Wayne had conferred in whispers before Wayne hopped out and Emrys drove up to the palace to sell his sheep.

She knew that Ishihara must have told Wayne something about the location of Hunter and Steve. Because she had not seen or heard any sign of them, she supposed Ishihara's enhanced hearing had brought him their voices in the distance. She had no real optimism that she could talk Ishihara into changing sides, but she decided to try raising some doubts again.

"The First Law was never intended for situations like this," Jane said quietly.

"What do you mean?" Ishihara asked. "I have kept you from harm."

"You're keeping me prisoner. I would be safer with Hunter. You already know that. I say you are violating the First Law by holding me now that Hunter has arrived."

"What form of harm are you suffering?"

"I'm being harmed simply by having to stay with you. It's not my choice."

"Wayne Nystrom will be harmed if his career is destroyed. I intend to balance his concerns with yours. Neither of you will suffer direct physical harm."

"Think about the intention of the First Law. Do you really believe that kidnapping was included?"

"To prevent a human from being harmed, it has been an option throughout the history of positronic robots. Otherwise, it would have been explicitly prohibited."

"I say you are wrong, Ishihara. Think about it." Jane spoke firmly but did not feel encouraged. Wayne had obviously given Ishihara some effective arguments of his own at some point and, after all, Wayne was also a roboticist.

Hunter found the maneuvers today to be a repeat of the day before. He put most of his effort into avoiding injuring his opponents. While he remained close to Steve, he observed that Steve learned very quickly and did not need specific help.

The day wore on uneventfully. Finally, late in the afternoon, Lucius ordered the troop back to the tor. When the weapons, armor, tack, and horses had been put away, Hunter and Steve walked back up to the village.

Steve looked up at him, grinning. "The trouble with this stuff is, the more time I spend riding and fighting, the more tired I get. The more time you spend out in the sunlight, the more energy you draw from your converters. Imagine what an army of robots could do here."

"We could not fight humans," said Hunter. "We would be useless as an army."

"I was just speculating. Think about it—"

"It makes me uncomfortable to consider it," Hunter said abruptly.

"All right. Sorry."

"Harriet called me again just now. She and one of the women she has met have gone for a walk in the village. We will look for them."

"Okay."

In the village, Hunter saw Harriet standing with a much younger woman by a stall that sold crockery. Before he and Steve reached them, however, Bedwyr walked out of the crowd, munching on a piece of bread. Steve had introduced him to Hunter last night before they had returned to the camp.

"Well, Hunter, how do you like your training?" Bedwyr turned to Steve. "You have no broken bones, I see."

"No, we are fine," said Hunter.

"Come with us," said Steve. "We're going to speak to a friend. We'll introduce you."

Bedwyr fell into step with them.

"Harriet!" Steve called cheerfully.

Harriet turned and waved.

"That's your friend?" Bedwyr's eyebrows rose. "She's with Gwenhyvaer."

"Did you say 'Guinevere'?" Steve asked in surprise.

"You say it oddly," said Bedwyr. "If you know the name, though, you must have heard. Rumor says Artorius will make her queen."

"She's just a kid," Steve muttered.

"She has her growth." Bedwyr laughed. "Not too young to become a queen, eh?"

"You know her?"

"Only by sight."

When they reached the stall, Harriet introduced Gwenhyvaer to Hunter and Steve. In turn, Steve introduced them both to Bedwyr. Gwenhyvaer nodded primly to them all and turned back to the crockery.

"We met Bedwyr in the village last night," said Steve. "We drank together."

"We won't see many taverns on the campaign," said Bedwyr, grinning.

"Are you from this area?" Harriet asked. "I wondered what it's like. We're from Linnuis."

"Yes, my village is not far. Half a day's ride. Life is good there. But we must send good men to ride with Artorius, or else the Saxons will have it all."

"Would you tell me about your village? Really tell me, I mean."

"As you wish, of course. I doubt it's much different from your own."

"Let's sit down somewhere and visit," said Steve. "What do you say, Hunter? After all that riding today, I'd like to relax."

"You go on," Gwenhyvaer said to Harriet. "After I browse some more, I'm going back to the palace. I'll remind the sentries to let you in."

"All right."

"I have no objection," said Hunter.

Wayne encouraged Emrys to leave the village at midday, while Hunter and Steve remained on maneuvers with the troop. He did not know for sure if Hunter would cooperate with his demands or not. However, he told Ishihara to keep a careful watch behind them as the cart left the tor, and Ishihara reported no sign that Hunter or Steve had followed them.

In the late afternoon, Emrys left the hut to hike

back to his son, tending the main flock. Wayne waited until Jane used the outhouse and was out of hearing. Then he approached Ishihara and spoke quietly.

"Hunter almost certainly spotted us leaving the tor," said Wayne. "He will know which direction we took. What do you think the chances are that he will risk trying to rescue Jane instead of catching MC 6 and trading him to me?"

"He has a great deal of room for interpretation of the First Law in this case," said Ishihara. "However, I believe that my presence gives him the freedom to move slowly."

"I think so, too. Without you, he would feel he had to rescue Jane right away because I can't protect her effectively alone. You can."

"Yes. Given that Hunter knows I must keep Jane from harm, he does not have to come for her immediately."

"When I spoke to Hunter, I got the impression that he accepted my terms," said Wayne. "He'll consider trading MC 6 to me for Jane. But I have to ask if you'll allow it. I don't know of any interpretation of the First Law that will cause you to prevent this deal. Do you?"

"No. As long as I protect you and Jane until the time that she is released directly to Hunter's care, I can cooperate with you in this."

"Good."

"I must offer another interpretation of Hunter's moves, however."

"What?"

"Hunter may not worry about Jane further, since he knows I must take care of her. He may just get MC 6 and forget about dealing with you for her."

"You think he can do that under the First Law?" Wayne frowned, gazing out over the cool, gray sky in the distance over Cadbury Tor.

"Perhaps. I cannot be certain. However, since MC 6 is the only component robot remaining at large, Hunter knows you will have no further interest in Jane if he simply takes MC 6 back to our time."

"You mean he'll figure you and I will just return, too, and let Jane go."

"He knows I cannot allow harm to come to Jane. That may free him to ignore your deal entirely."

Wayne drew in a long, slow breath and let it out again. "I must proceed on the assumption that the First Law will pressure him to act more aggressively toward Jane. To that end, I may instruct you to remain here with Jane while I return to Cadbury. Will this be acceptable under your interpretation of the First Law?"

"I do not like separating from you. I must protect you, as well."

"In the absence of a clear danger under the First Law, you should have no problem. Cadbury will be safe for me. Do you agree?"

"Yes." Ishihara lowered his voice. "If you wish this to remain private, we must change the subject. Jane is coming back."

Hunter sat down in a small tavern with Bedwyr, Harriet, and Steve. Harriet asked Bedwyr many detailed questions about life in his village; Hunter could hear the historian behind her questions. Steve listened politely, sipping from a goblet of mead, sprawled back in his seat comfortably.

A bell began to ring loudly, clearly, and rhythmically outside. Bedwyr promptly put his goblet down on the table and got up. Then he looked in surprise at the others, who had not moved.

The other patrons in the tavern, and the tavern-keeper, hurried out the door.

"It's the village bell," he said. "Aren't you coming? Important news must have come."

Steve started to get up.

"No," said Hunter, gently placing a hand on Steve's arm. "Please inform us of the news."

"As you wish." Bedwyr shrugged and hurried out of the tavern.

Outside, Hunter heard many feet from all over the village moving quickly up and down the streets.

"What's wrong, Hunter?" Steve asked.

"The three of us have not had a chance to confer freely for some time," said Hunter. "We can talk now and find out what the news is later."

"Well, what do you want to talk about?" Steve set down his goblet.

"If MC 6 has not returned to full size, or if we cannot find any clue to his location, Steve and I may have to consider leaving the troop we have joined. If we do, I judge that we cannot expect to be welcome in the village any longer. Is this accurate?"

"Yes, if you just quit or disappear," said Harriet thoughtfully. "No army tolerates deserters, though in this time, organization is not very formal. Quitting now probably would mean that you would simply not be welcome back. Deserting on campaign, however, is likely a hanging offense. But I wonder if you can arrange to be reassigned to garrison duty here in the tor."

"Is that likely?" Hunter asked.

"No. New arrivals are not likely to be trusted. But I can ask Gwenhyvaer if she can help."

"If we go out on campaign, we could be wasting valuable time," said Hunter. "But suppose this is necessary. Will you be safe here?"

"Yes. Gwenhyvaer seems to like me. And if my husband has gone out to fight with Artorius, I will look better to everyone in the palace."

"I asked a couple of sentries last night if they had seen anyone of MC 6's description in the palace," said Steve. "I guess if you'd heard anything like that, you would have said so already."

"Yes, I would have." Harriet shook her head. "MC 6 may not be in the palace, though. He could be working in the village during the day and either spending the night hidden away in the village or out in the countryside nearby."

"He could still be microscopic," said Hunter. "We are searching in a relatively small area with a modest population. If he had returned to full size and had remained in the village, we should have found someone who has seen him by now."

"We haven't offered a reward here, like we have before," said Steve.

"I can do that," said Harriet. "If I remain here to cover the village, then you can see if he appears with the riders at some point."

"You seem very comfortable here," said Hunter.

"Hunter, I might as well tell you something," said Harriet slowly. "As I mentioned before, I do not believe in chaos theory at all. I'm willing to fulfill my commitment to you in finding MC 6, but then I want to stay in this time."

"Forever?" Steve sat up in his chair, startled. "Are you crazy?"

"Maybe." Harriet smiled. "But I used to dream about living in this time—the focus of my profes-

From the R. Hunter Files

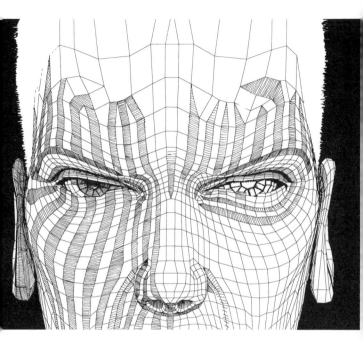

The now-famous prototype of the highly successful "Hunter" class robot first demonstrated his
remarkable abilities in the Mojave Center
Governor case. The following images are drawn
from the Robot City archives of Derec Avery, the
eminent robotics historian

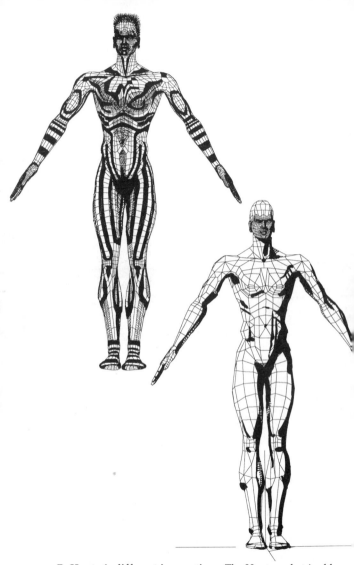

R. Hunter's different incarnations. The Hunter robot is able to assume different forms, including those pictured here: human form, standard robot mode, and full battle array.

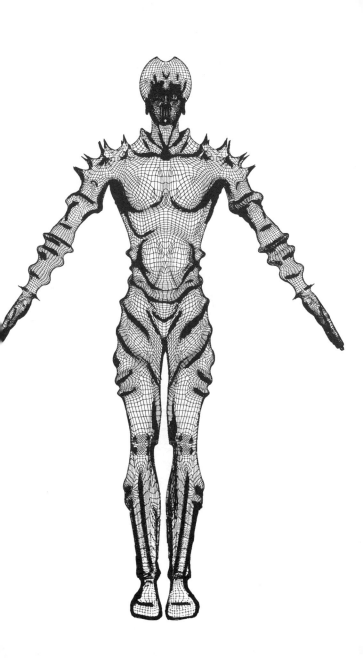

MC robots merged. The final independent component of MC Governor is captured by R. Hunter in the distant past and merged with the remaining five.

The Bohung Institute. A security robot patrols the Institute's perimeter.

MC Governor confronts R. Hunter. Following MC Governor's capture and reintegration, R. Hunter confronts him in his office.

King Artorius. Flanked by R. Hunter and Steve, the king prepares for battle.

Cadbury Castle. The primary base of Artorius's men, this castle is the basis of the Camelot legend.

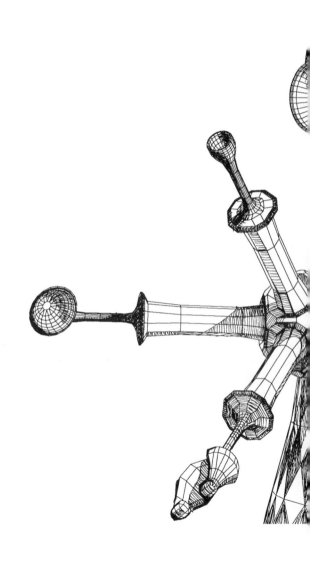

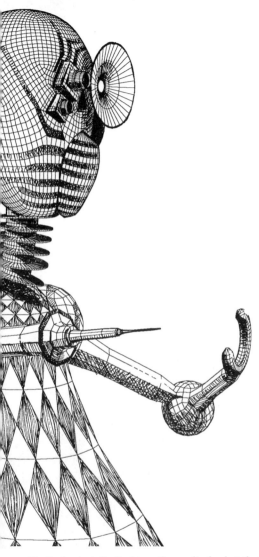

Medical robot. R. Cushing, the medical robot that provided vaccinations and treatments for R. Hunter's team for all their journeys.

Room F-12. The time travel apparatus used by both R. Hunter and his teams and Wayne Nystrom and R. Ishihara to chase MC Governor is guarded by R. Daladier and another security robot, in the event that Nystrom returns.

Observing the Saxon soldiers. Bedwyr joins R. Hunter and Steve in observing the movements of the Saxon troops.

sional research. And when Hunter told me about the mission to travel back in time, I knew I wanted to do it."

"You accepted this job with the intention of staying here?" Hunter asked.

"Yes. I admit it. But I waited to make my final decision until after I had seen what my prospects would be. Since I have the advantage of hindsight, I can use it to improve my chances. For instance, I know before Gwenhyvaer and Artorius themselves that they will marry. I intend to position myself as a mentor and friend to her. After my husband disappears, maybe in battle against the Saxons, I will be an honored widow. I hope she will accept me as a personal servant."

Hunter said nothing. On the second mission, which took the team to Jamaica in the seventeenth century to capture MC 2, he had hired a historian named Rita Chavez. Rita had decided to go out on her own only on impulse, after the team had arrived there. Her leaving the team had endangered the mission, but she had eventually changed her mind and returned to the team. Harriet remained willing to fulfill her duties, apparently, but she seemed to have made a much more calm and studied decision not to return to their own time.

"Have you really thought this through?" Steve demanded. "What kind of doctors do they have here? What happens if you get sick, or get hurt?"

"Yes, I've thought it through. I'm not one to romanticize this era—if anything, I know it better than most people from our time."

"Before we left, you said this was a time of social and political transition," said Hunter. "The border between the Britons and the Saxons fluctuates. Why do you want to live in a time that is so unstable?"

"In terms of scholarly study, this time is unstable. Very little from these years will last for as long as another century, when the Saxons conquer and settle throughout all of what will become England. But for one middle-aged woman like me, life in a village far from the military front will be very routine, day in and day out."

"What will you do when the Saxons come?" Steve frowned. "That time can't be very routine."

"Again, I'm using the advantage of historical hindsight. The efforts of Artorius and his men will hold off the Saxons for the rest of my lifetime. My presence won't change that. Even under the worst circumstances, I'll be gone before the Saxons reach this area."

Hunter did not respond. The First Law required him to take Harriet back both for her own safety and because of his own belief in chaos theory. The harm to her in returning would be virtually nonexistent, yet in his opinion, the potential harm to the future if she stayed remained very large. If necessary, he would take her back under duress, and he did not want to tell her that; she might decide to run away, as Rita had. In any case, this matter would have to wait until the team was ready to leave this time again.

Bedwyr ran back into the tavern, out of breath. Behind him, Hunter could see other people running through the street. Shouts came from all over the village.

"What is it?" Steve asked, looking up.

"A scouting patrol just came back from the Saxon border." Bedwyr paused to catch his breath. "A new fleet of Saxons has crossed the Channel. With their brethren already in Britain, they are preparing to march soon."

"What will Artorius do?" Hunter asked.

"He already came out to speak. That's why the bell rang. He has issued orders for us to march tomorrow."

"Most of his army is not here," said Hunter.

"That's right," said Bedwyr. "His personal troop and Lucius's green recruits are the only ones. But couriers are being sent to the countryside to tell all the veterans to meet us on our line of march."

"Can they arrive in time?" Steve asked.

"Of course." Bedwyr laughed. "Remember, we are all mounted. The Saxons march on their own sorry feet. We will gather long before we meet them."

"When do we leave?" Hunter asked. "Tonight?"

"No, no. Attack is not imminent, only the need to open the campaign. The baggage train must be assembled and that work will go on late into the night. In the morning, we will ride."

Hunter turned to Harriet. "Will you be welcome in the palace indefinitely? If not, we must find another place for you. We should begin now."

"I'll talk to Gwenhyvaer about it right away," said Harriet, standing. "She must have heard the bell, too. I imagine the whole palace is buzzing."

"What about us?" Steve asked Bedwyr. "Do we have to report to the camp right away?"

"Of course not!" Bedwyr laughed and sat down in his chair again. "Every man not on sentry duty will be coming to the taverns soon! It's our last night of freedom! Now where's that tavernkeeper—still out in the street?"

Jane knelt by the fire, setting out bowls on the hearth. Just as Ygerna began to ladle mutton stew into the bowls, hoofbeats sounded outside. Emrys and Ishihara went out into the twilight to see who was coming. Wayne remained on a stool near the door, which was left ajar.

Ygerna paid no attention as she ladled out the stew. Jane feigned disinterest but listened carefully. A single horse cantered right up to the front of the hut.

"Does anyone here ride with Artorius?" An unfamiliar man's voice called out.

"No," said Emrys. "Why?"

"Artorius rides tomorrow! Spread the word to

anyone who rides with him. The Saxons are marching!" The hoofbeats cantered away.

Emrys came back inside. At the same moment,
Wayne got up and slipped outside, blocking Ishihara
from entering. He closed the door behind him.

"I sold my sheep just in time." Emrys grinned.
"Did you hear?"

"Artorius rides tomorrow," said Ygerna. "That's
good. He will defeat the Saxons again this year."

"The other shepherds will have to leave at dawn
to drive their sheep to the tor," said Emrys, coming
to take a bowl of stew from Ygerna. "Even then,
they may not arrive until after he has left. If they
want to sell their sheep to him after that, they will
have to chase the baggage train."

Jane tensed, wondering what this would mean
to her. If Hunter and Steve had to maintain the
goodwill of those around them, she supposed they
would have to go. She knew that Wayne was confer-
ring with Ishihara at that moment about the same
question. They would have to decide what to do and,
in particular, what to do with her.

The central issue remained the same as before,
the whereabouts of MC 6. If MC 6 went on campaign
with Artorius, then Hunter and Steve would also
go. Wayne could not possibly find out if MC 6 was
going before tomorrow, but he might decide that if
Hunter went, he should go.

Jane tried to figure out what Ishihara would do if
Wayne decided to follow Artorius. In her judgment,
Ishihara could neither let Wayne follow a troop of
riders going to war alone, nor could he leave Jane
here indefinitely. Therefore, Ishihara would have to
take her, too.

She still did not know for sure if Hunter and

Steve would go with Artorius or attempt something else.

Early the next morning, Steve sat by the campfire next to Hunter, eating a bowl of hot cereal. The night before, Hunter had told Steve that Harriet had called him to report that Gwenhyvaer would give her lodging for as long as her husband was gone on campaign. Now, everyone around them spoke excitedly of riding out today. As soon as each squad had finished breakfast, they put out their fire and hurried to the other side of the tor to prepare their horses.

When Cynric led his squad around the slope, Steve moved close to Hunter and spoke quietly.

"You want to take one more quick walk through the village? If MC 6 isn't going with Artorius, either microscopically or at full size, we really are wasting our time."

"I dare not," said Hunter. "We must maintain our standing here."

This time, as the riders lined up to get their tack and their weapons, teamsters hitched horses to wagons. Baggage handlers loaded spare weapons and armor into some of them. Some teamsters drove empty wagons up to the village; others drove loaded wagons back.

"I see MC 6," said Hunter softly, looking out over the slope from his place in line.

"What? Where?" Steve fought to remain calm. "Maybe we can get him before we leave."

"He is riding in the back of the second wagon coming down the slope from the village."

"Yeah, I guess I see him now. I couldn't have recognized him for sure at this distance." Steve hesitated. "You're sure that's him?"

"Yes. When we see where the wagon goes, we can decide whether or not to approach it immediately."

"You mean, we'll just grab him right now?" Steve asked in surprise.

"We should move as soon as we can do so safely and successfully."

"But what about Jane? We can't grab MC 6 and just walk away from here to get her. If we don't jump right back to our own time, we'll have to go on campaign. And if that's the case, I don't think we should alert MC 6 to the fact that we're after him."

"We must take MC 6 immediately back to their own time, leave him securely in MC Governor's office, and then come back for Jane."

"What about Wayne's threat?" Steve asked. "He can order Ishihara away from Jane, so she won't be protected."

"Our first responsibility remains returning MC 6 to our own time. Further, I do not believe that Wayne truly would endanger Jane. I judge him to be a man who would threaten this in the hope of influencing me under the First Law, but who would not carry out the threat."

"I'm not so sure."

The wagon in which MC 6 rode pulled up near the main gate of the outer rampart, behind some other loaded wagons.

"We're moving to the front of the line," said Steve. "Are we going to get our tack first, or just go now?"

"We should waste no more time," said Hunter decisively. "Come."

Hunter stepped out of the line and angled quickly across the slope, down toward the loaded wagons. Most of the teamsters sat holding the reins, simply waiting, but a few of them stood on the ground, adjusting harnesses or ropes holding cargo.

"Can't he tell somehow that you're a robot?" Steve asked. "Didn't we have to consider this on earlier missions, too? What did we do?"

"If he studies me with magnified vision or hearing, he will detect that I do not have human skin or a heartbeat. We must gamble that he will not bother, since he has no reason to expect another robot here in this century."

"Oh, yeah. That's right."

Steve followed Hunter, keeping an eye on MC 6. The component robot sat in the rear of a wagon watching his surroundings alertly, but of course he had no idea that Hunter and Steve had come from their time to get him. He glanced at them casually and then looked past them, toward the paddock.

"Since he is not afraid of us, we can walk right up and speak to him," said Hunter. "Give him a direct instruction to cooperate fully with us."

"What do we do after we get him?" Steve asked. "We don't want to vanish with him in front of these other people. What should I say?"

"Your second instruction must be to jump down out of the wagon and come around behind it with us. we will hurry out the main gate. As soon as we turn the corner and stand out of sight, I will trigger the belt unit."

"Got it." Steve glanced at the gate, just on the other side of the wagon, and looked at MC 6 again.

"Ho! You there! What do you want?"

Steve stopped, startled. Hunter turned in surprise. A tall, burly man wearing a tanned leather tunic marched up to them. He scowled through a bushy brown beard.

"I say, what do you want here?"

"We must have a moment with this man," Hunter said firmly, gesturing toward MC 6. "Who are you?"

"I am Gaius, the wagonmaster." He glared suspiciously at Hunter. "What do you want with him? He doesn't speak British or Latin. The only way we can communicate with him is through gestures."

"We speak his language," said Hunter.

Steve almost called out to MC 6 in English, to order him to cooperate. He thought better of it, realizing that they might not get a chance to take MC 6 away from the sight of the wagonmaster. In that event, he did not want to alert MC 6 to the fact that they had come from his time to take him back.

"And I asked, what do you want with him?" Before Hunter could answer, Gaius turned to MC 6. "You know these men?" He jerked a thumb toward Hunter.

MC 6 looked back and forth between them. He obviously did not understand the question. He shrugged lightly, shaking his head.

"You men get back to your horses," said Gaius angrily. "Now. I have wagons to line up." He moved to block Hunter's path to MC 6.

Hunter turned and walked back up the slope. Steve hurried to keep alongside. At least they had not revealed their true intentions to MC 6.

Jane said nothing about Wayne's plans the next morning. She helped Ygerna tend the fire, waiting to see what Wayne and Ishihara were going to do. They all ate breakfast, the same hot cereal as every other morning. Then Wayne and Ishihara stepped outside again, this time with Emrys.

The suspense for Jane finally ended when Ishihara came back inside alone.

"Emrys will drive us to the village again today," Ishihara said to Jane. "Wayne instructed me to explain that we must search for an acquaintance there. Emrys expressed his gratitude again for my help in cutting the firewood and, by chance, causing him to drive his sheep to sell before his neighbors. So he will send his eldest son to tend the flock again and help us today, as well."

Jane nodded. She did not want Ishihara or Wayne to know that she was glad to be going, too. On her way out of the hut, she gave Ygerna a quick smile and pat on the shoulder. Jane hoped to join Hunter somehow today, which would mean she would not be back, but of course she could hardly say so.

This time, Emrys did not have firewood to load or sheep to drive. Ygerna gave them some bread and cold cooked mutton to take with them, wrapped first in a clean cloth, then put into a heavier cloth bag. Ishihara lifted Jane into the back of the empty cart, as before, and climbed in with her. Emrys waited for Wayne to join him in the front, then shook the reins and started out.

Today, other shepherds with their flocks clogged the road to the tor. Most of them walked, with a dog or two to drive the sheep. A few others also drove mule carts, carrying either butchered carcasses or, in some cases, an entire family going for an outing.

Emrys, the only shepherd without sheep or a full

cart, drove a little faster. With a big grin, he waved
to some of his friends as he drew near, calling out
greetings occasionally. He drove off the road to pass
them and their flocks, taking the cart over the sod
on one side or the other.

Jane watched the tor closely, hoping to arrive
before the riders left the tor. Today, however, they
did not make it. The troop rode out well ahead
of their arrival. Instead of breaking formation to
begin maneuvers, however, the troop rode straight
out along a different road, one that angled eastward
across the rolling hills.

When she saw they were leaving, she tensed,
hoping to spot whether Hunter and Steve rode with
them. She did not see either of them, though she
realized they might be lost in the crowd of riders.
However, she decided that even if she spotted Hunter by his height, she could not risk trying to attract
his attention from this distance. Hunter might not
hear her and Wayne would get angry at the attempt.
She wanted to reserve her efforts for a move that
would work.

Ishihara saw Hunter's head and shoulders towering above his companions, as he rode with the troop away from the tor, well ahead of Emrys's cart. Since Wayne had told him not to alert Jane unnecessarily to new information regarding Hunter, Ishihara merely leaned forward between Emrys and Wayne and pointed with one finger toward the riders. Wayne nodded.

After the riders had passed from the main gate, Ishihara watched a long train of wagons follow the riders out of the tor and up the road to the east. Over twenty men and women trudged behind it, failing to keep up. For a while, Ishihara, Wayne, and Emrys continued to ride in silence. As the cart reached the main gate of the tor, after the baggage train had moved far up the road, Wayne leaned close to Ishihara.

"Who are those people walking behind the wagons?" Wayne asked.

"I believe they are called camp followers. The women are following the soldiers and the men are scavengers, hoping to loot the dead after a battle.

As the army marches, more of them will probably see it and follow, too."

"Do you agree that we have to follow them all, too?" Wayne whispered. The sound of the mule's hooves helped camouflage his voice from Jane in the back of the cart.

"Yes," Ishihara whispered back. "I judge that Hunter and Steve would not go on this campaign unless they knew that MC 6 was also going."

"How can we arrange to go, too?"

Ishihara turned to Emrys.

"We must ask you for help once again."

"What is it?"

"We would like to borrow your wagon," said Ishihara. "For a few days, at least. Maybe more."

"What do you want with it?"

"We must follow a couple of friends who have left with Artorius."

"You want to follow Artorius on campaign? That will take more than a few days. He could be gone until the leaves turn in autumn."

Wayne could not understand British, so he looked back and forth between them for a clue to Emrys's answer.

"I can guarantee we will bring it back as soon as possible," said Ishihara.

"But I may need it before you return." Emrys shook his head. "You have done me several kindnesses, but I will need my cart. Maybe we can find another way for you and your friends to follow Artorius."

"What do you mean?" Ishihara asked.

"Well, I could drive you to the baggage train. They always need men to work on the wagons during a campaign. During the summer, some may go too close to the battle and get killed; others run away to find something else."

"What did he say?" Wayne asked.

Ishihara switched to English. "He won't let us borrow his wagon. Instead, he suggested that he take us to the baggage train and we can earn our keep."

"If Hunter saw us, we'd be helpless. He would take Jane and me."

"I cannot allow it, anyway. The danger to Jane is too great in that sort of company."

"Yeah."

Ishihara changed languages again. "We dare not take Jane to the baggage train. We need to find our own wagon or mounts to ride."

"I understand," said Emrys. "And you want to be able to return on your own, as well, without having to walk."

"Yes."

Emrys looked across the slope. Then, without a word, he shook the reins and drove the cart at an angle up the tor. They left the road leading up to the village.

Ishihara saw the paddock and two other buildings ahead of them. Only two animals remained in the pen and he supposed they had been left behind because they were not suitable to ride. He did not see any small carts similar to Emrys's.

As Emrys drew up in front of the paddock, a short, stocky man wearing a ragged leather tunic walked on a wooden crutch under his left arm from one of the buildings.

"If you want to sell something, you're too late," said the man with the crutch. "You'll have to catch up to the baggage train."

"No, no. We wish to buy," said Emrys. "Are you the master of horse?"

"Of course not." The man scowled. "The master of horse has gone with Artorius. So has the armorer. I am Antonius." He hesitated. "What do you want to buy?"

"A couple of horses," said Ishihara.

"The price of a good horse goes up this time of year," said Antonius.

"Nonsense," said Emrys. "Every good horse has already been taken. You have none at all."

"Then what do you want here?"

"I will dicker with the man who can sell," said Emrys. "If you are not the master of horse, who makes the decisions here now?"

"Well, until Artorius returns, I do."

"We want two or three mounts to ride on the road."

"Just to travel? Not to join the cavalry or to pull a wagon?"

"No."

"All right. Come and look."

Emrys and Ishihara got down and followed Antonius into the paddock. Wayne hopped down and watched but did not bother to enter the pen. Jane stayed where she was.

Antonius led Emrys and Ishihara to a pair of small, brown mules standing quietly. Ishihara noticed their long ears and white noses. Both animals placidly watched them approach.

Emrys looked over the mules carefully. He patted them and stroked their legs and necks as he walked around them. Then he examined their teeth.

Finally, Emrys took some coins out of a pouch and held them out to Antonius.

The other man leaned on his crutch and frowned, shaking his head.

Without speaking, Emrys took out one more coin and held it out.

Antonius shook his head again.

"That is all he is worth," said Emrys.

Antonius said nothing.

Emrys dropped the coins back into his pouch and walked away. Ishihara followed him. Just as they reached the gate of the paddock, Antonius began hustling after them awkwardly on his crutch.

"All right," Antonius called. "He is yours."

Emrys turned and spilled the coins carefully into his palm again. He dropped them into Antonius's outstretched hand. Then Antonius walked back to the storage building and came out with an old bridle and a long rope. In the paddock again, he tossed them to Emrys, who slipped the bridle on one of the mules and tied the rope to rings on the bridle to use as reins. Then he led the mule out of the paddock.

"I ask only that you return it to me when you come back," said Emrys, holding the reins out to Ishihara.

"That might not be possible," said Ishihara, without accepting the reins. "If we have to act quickly, returning it could endanger me."

"I know the campaign could be dangerous. Please take care of yourselves." Emrys placed the reins in Ishihara's hands. "You are . . . unusual friends."

"Thank you. We shall bring the mule back if we are able." Ishihara turned and related this to Wayne, knowing that Jane could overhear him.

"All right, but it's only one mule for three of us," said Jane.

"What else can we do?" Ishihara asked.

"Nothing," said Wayne. "We have no money."

"What's wrong with this mule?" Jane demanded.

"What do you mean?" Wayne asked.

"Why didn't they take him to ride? Or for the baggage train? Is he old or something?"

"Antonius explained," said Ishihara. "This mule is young and healthy but too small to put in harness. The warriors disdain riding a mule into battle and they have enough food, so no one would want to eat it."

"I have another suspicion, too," Wayne added, lowering his voice.

"What?" Jane asked, concerned. "Something bad about the mule?"

"No, nothing like that." Wayne shook his head. "Since Antonius is in charge here for now, I think he's going to pocket the coins Emrys paid him. So if he sells a cavalry mule and keeps all the profit, he'll be happy enough."

"I am sure that Emrys cannot buy another," said Ishihara. "However, you and Wayne can ride this one together, bareback. He will tire more quickly than a horse carrying one rider, but the teams pulling the baggage train will tire quickly, too. We should be able to catch up tonight after they stop to make camp."

Jane nodded. "And you'll jog along beside us."

"Yes."

Jane climbed out of the cart. Emrys handed her the bag of bread and mutton. She accepted it.

"Thank you, Emrys," Jane said, in Latin. "Farewell."

Emrys understood her meaning, if not the words, and nodded politely.

"This won't last us very long," said Jane, turning to Ishihara. "What else are we going to eat on the way? This might last us two small meals, but tomorrow morning, we'll be on the road somewhere."

"If necessary, we can always use the belt unit to jump to another time and place for food," said Wayne. "But if we're lucky, we'll find MC 6 tonight, get him to come with us, and be done with the whole mess."

"All right," said Jane reluctantly. "I know you don't want to starve, either. But now that I think about it, what about getting through the night? If you don't get MC 6 to follow you tonight, we'll freeze out on the road without some kind of bedrolls."

"We must find blankets in the village," said Ishihara. "However, without money to buy them, we can only ask for Emrys to help again. I do not know how much more he will be willing and able to help."

"Maybe he can afford old ones," said Jane. "Their condition won't matter, as long as they don't have bugs or anything. Please ask him."

Ishihara turned to Emrys again. "Can we buy old, inexpensive blankets in the village? We can return them, too, with the mule."

"Of course," said Emrys. "I know which booth to visit. I can help with that. You will need a small pot in which to heat water, too."

"We will go to the village," said Ishihara. "Then, if our search for blankets succeeds, we will hurry on our way up the road."

Steve enjoyed riding out with Artorius's cavalry, in a column of four abreast. He rode on the far right of his rank, with Hunter on his immediate left and Cynric on Hunter's other side. Another member of their squad rode on the far left, with the remainder in the ranks behind them.

All of Lucius's troop of green recruits rode in the rear. No dust roiled up, however, because of the dampness in the earth. Overhead, gray clouds drifted across the sky.

Around him, Steve could see the excitement in the young faces of the other riders. The thought of going to war against the hated Saxons dominated their attention. None of them spoke now.

Up ahead, as the column drew away from Cadbury, the squads in the van cantered ahead of the rest. When the vanguard had opened some distance, the entire column was ordered to canter. Steve understood and kicked his mount; Artorius, already a veteran leader, wanted his men to vent their tension.

When the column slowed to a walk again, Steve could see the difference. The riders around him relaxed, breathless, and began talking and laughing among themselves. Under the hooves of the horses ahead, the soft road quickly turned to muddy slop, but no one cared. The road wound east and sometimes northeast around rolling hills covered with lush green grass; clumps of trees lined the hollows among the hills.

"I hear word from up ahead," said Hunter. "A rumor of our destination is slowly passing back through the column, from one man to another."

"Well, what is it? Where are we going?"

"To the River Dubglas in Linnuis," said Hunter. He lowered his voice and leaned toward Steve, switching to English. "According to the library data

I took before we left, that is the Douglas River in modern Lincolnshire."

"River Dubglas, you say?" Cynric, riding on the far side of Hunter from Steve, nodded. "That sounds right."

"So I heard," said Hunter.

"We fought them by the banks of that river late last season," said Cynric. "If we hope to drive them back this summer, we'll have to attack their territory. Last year's campaign penned them on the far side of the river, but I suppose they look to cross it again, with their reinforcements from across the Channel." His face tightened as he considered this.

"How long will we take to reach River Dubglas?" Hunter asked.

"If we ride without a break to the same site as last year's battle, three days. Our scouts will ride back with word as we draw closer, though, to tell Artorius exactly where on the river to go. We might spend some time moving up and down the bank. Artorius will make his final plans according to how many of our veterans join us quickly."

"You feel he may order us to wait and gather his troops before moving into battle?" Hunter asked.

"Anything is possible. We will find out his plans when we are close enough for our scouts to bring fresh information."

Steve understood the real questions in Hunter's mind, behind his spoken words. Hunter wanted to take Steve away from the column before any battle began. Ideally, they would find MC 6 and simply return together to their own time before the fighting started. Now Hunter could estimate that they had a minimum of three days before Artorius could reach the Saxons.

Wayne and Jane rode the mule. He held the reins while Jane sat behind him with her arms around his waist. Even at a walk, the mule's long legs moved faster than a human's legs would walk.

Ishihara had to stride quickly to keep up. He moved at a pace that no human could maintain for long, but of course had no trouble with it himself. Because the road had been churned to a deep muddy soup by the horses ahead, Wayne rode through the long grass by the side of the road.

In late morning, they caught up to the camp followers hiking after the riders. Ishihara led Wayne on a long detour around the camp followers, far enough to avoid conversation. Then they moved back to the side of the road again.

At midday, Wayne stopped for a break. He and Jane ate part of their bread and mutton in silence. Then they mounted again and continued on their journey.

Late in the afternoon, Ishihara suddenly trotted about twenty meters ahead of the mule, then stopped. As Wayne caught up to him, Ishihara raised a hand for him to halt. Wayne saw that Ishihara was listening to something.

"They have stopped to make camp," Ishihara said finally. "The noises are faint, but we will come within sight of the camp soon. We must decide how to proceed now, before anyone in the camp sees us."

"Well . . . I don't know exactly what to do," said Wayne. "What do you suggest?"

Ishihara looked up the road, which still wound through rolling hills ahead. "That long line of trees suggests a river or at least a stream that provides water for Artorius's camp. We will need water, too, so we might as well go close enough to see what the camp looks like."

"Yeah. Maybe we can see MC 6 from a distance." Wayne kicked the mule forward.

As Wayne passed, Ishihara looked behind him, at Jane. "You are still well?"

"Yeah," Jane muttered.

The troops halted to make camp by a small stream. Hunter saw new scouting patrols ride out, crossing the stream. He understood that by stopping with plenty of daylight left, the main column allowed the baggage train time to catch up before darkness fell.

The squads split up and fanned out from the road. The riders tended their horses first, unsaddling them and hobbling them to graze. Then the men were ordered to gather firewood to make separate campfires for the night.

"There's dead wood among those live trees, all over the place," said Steve, glancing at the trees lining the stream. "We don't need everybody to gather it."

"Every man does his share," growled Cynric. "Come on, you two."

"Hold it," called Bedwyr, with a big grin. He walked briskly among the other men and horses toward them. "I have business here, Cynric. How did my green friends fare on their first day of march?"

"Very well, thank you," said Hunter.

"You told me you lead a scouting patrol," said Steve. "Do you have any news? We heard a rumor about going to River Dubglas."

"Yes, that's right," said Bedwyr. "But none of the patrols today have made contact with the Saxons. Fresh patrols rode out a few minutes ago, but we're still a long way from Linnuis."

Steve nodded.

"I have a serious reason to speak with you," said Bedwyr. "Artorius is worried about having so many green recruits and so few veterans. The rest of our veterans should join us during the next day or so, but he wants to mix some quick-witted new recruits with his veterans to give them some experience. I want you two to join my patrol."

"Really?" Steve grinned but glanced uncertainly at Hunter. "That sounds exciting."

"It can be," said Bedwyr.

Hunter considered the offer quickly. On the face of it, scouting could be more dangerous to Steve than riding in the body of the army, since the patrols would make the first contact with the enemy. They could even be ambushed. However, Hunter also had to prepare for them both to leave the area before any fighting began, ideally without witnesses. Slipping away from the rest of the patrol momentarily would be much easier than leaving the main column. He knew that scouts occasionally were killed and never accounted for on campaigns of this sort, so no one would question their disappearance. In fact, when he and Steve had to return for Jane, they might claim simply to have lost their way or to have been caught behind the enemy lines for a short time.

"We accept," said Hunter.

"Ah! I'm glad. We'll do well together. Get your gear and your horses."

Cynric sighed loudly. "All right." He jerked a thumb toward Hunter. "His weight is rough on a horse, but he's good with both his horse and his weapons." He glanced at Steve and Hunter. "Watch yourselves out front, there." Then he trudged after the men going to gather firewood.

Steve looked toward the rear, where the baggage train had rolled into view down the muddy road. "Bedwyr, would you help us with a personal matter? After we move our horses and belongings up to join your patrol?"

"What is it?"

"We, uh, have to confront a man in the baggage train. We don't want him to get away, and the wagonmaster stopped us from seeing him before we left."

"The same man you were looking for in the palace, when we met?"

"Maybe. He ... owes us a little money." Steve grinned. "We want it back."

Bedwyr laughed. "You told me before he did not owe you any money."

Steve had forgotten what he had told Bedwyr before, and now had to explain the discrepancy. "Well, you and I had just met. I, uh ..."

"You wanted to be careful until you learned what kind of friend I might be." Bedwyr chuckled. "Of course I understand. And on this matter of finding your friend, I will be glad to help you. But what do you want me for?"

"Maybe you will know some of the men. We won't be total strangers."

"Yes, that would be good. I will go with you. And I know Gaius, the wagonmaster. But first they will have to catch up and break formation to make camp."

"I promise we will commit no violence," said Hunter. "We only wish to speak to him, preferably alone. We need just a moment."

By the time Hunter and Steve led their mounts to the place where Bedwyr's patrol had stopped, the baggage train had halted behind the main column. Bedwyr introduced Hunter and Steve to their new companions in the patrol. Then they walked back through the camp to the baggage train.

The men in the wagon crews jumped off to unload. Hunter spotted MC 6 just as he hopped from the wagon; when he reached the ground, he was hidden by other wagons. Teamsters began unhitching the teams.

"I saw him for a moment." Hunter pointed in the direction of MC 6.

"Good," said Steve.

Bedwyr moved up to lead the way.

"Hey, you there! Halt." Gaius blocked Bedwyr's path. "What do you want here, Bedwyr? Shouldn't you be out looking for Saxons?"

"Easy, Gaius." Bedwyr smiled pleasantly. "My friends and I have business with one of your men. It won't take long." He started to walk around the other man.

Gaius stepped sideways to block his way. "I remember them from this morning. Get back to your places, all of you. We have work to do."

"We have no wish to disturb anyone," said Hunter. "Our business will take only a moment."

"Not while we're making camp, it won't." Gaius glanced west, up at the sun. "We barely have the daylight we need now. Go on!"

Some other men had come up behind Gaius.

"Easy, friend," said Bedwyr, still smiling. "No one will interfere with your work. We only want a quick word with one man."

"Get out!" Gaius shouted, pointing back the way they had come.

Hunter considered forcing his way past the wagonmaster and taking MC 6 by brute strength. Bedwyr might not join him, but Steve would. However, even if they were successful, that move would force Hunter to flee back with Steve and MC 6 to their own time in front of many witnesses, risking a significant change in the tales they would tell. Obviously, Steve and the men of this time might be unnecessarily injured in the altercation. In addition, Hunter had to consider that the sheer number of men in front of him might prevent him from pushing his way through, since he would not display more than human strength to them. He might simply create bad feeling without apprehending MC 6. Hunter decided to postpone their approach to MC 6 again.

"Never mind, Bedwyr," Hunter said quietly. He turned, followed by Steve and Bedwyr.

"He's really a good man," said Bedwyr, as they walked. "Too many of the warriors treat his men arrogantly, as though being a fighter is more important. Gaius knows this isn't true and is very protective of them."

"I have to admit, I kind of like him," said Steve. "He's direct and businesslike."

"Perhaps we can approach our friend again later," said Hunter. "When the wagon crews have finished their work. Bedwyr, what do you think?"

"Not tonight. Gaius doesn't like being pushed. Maybe I can think of a favor to do for him."

"What kind of favor?" Steve asked.

"Well, if we chanced across a nice deer, for instance, on our patrol tomorrow, or a few good game birds, we might share our luck with him. In turn, he would share it with his men, and owe us a favor in return."

"I understand," said Hunter.

"For now, let's get back up to the patrol," said Bedwyr. "I'm ready for dinner."

Jane stood next to the mule in a small clump of trees. Wayne, on the ground next to her, held its reins. with Ishihara, they watched the wagons of the baggage train from a distance. They could see Hunter's head and shoulders over a crowd of men in front of the wagons.

"I can't hear them," said Wayne. "What are they saying to each other?"

"Hunter and Steve claim they want to get some money from a man working in the baggage train," said Ishihara. "I surmise that this is MC 6. They have a local man named Bedwyr helping them."

Jane kept looking, but she could still only see Hunter's head and shoulders from this distance. Steve remained lost in the crowd. Like Wayne, she could not make out the conversation, though she heard a low rumble of voices.

"You mean they're about to get him already?" Wayne's shoulders sagged.

"No. The wagonmaster, Gaius, has refused to let them pass. He does not want anyone interfering with his wagon crews while they are making camp."

"Hunter's turning around," said Wayne. "Is he just giving up?"

"For the moment, he has agreed to leave. However, this provides us with information. I have not spotted MC 6 yet, but now we know where to look for him."

"Let's go," said Wayne. "Quick, before Hunter sneaks back somehow. He won't give up for long. Maybe we can just run in and get MC 6 right away."

"I do not recommend it," said Ishihara. "In fact, I strongly suggest that we do nothing at the moment."

"Why?" Wayne demanded. "We know where he is, and he's not very far away."

"Gaius was adamant about not allowing anyone to disturb his crews. Some of his men stood behind him, and from their posture I believe they were ready to fight if necessary. They are likely to remain angry."

"Oh." Wayne sighed, still looking at the men around the wagons. "I see what you mean. I hate waiting, but if we can't get to him anyway, then we should lie low. We don't want to alert Hunter or MC 6 to our presence."

"In the meantime, we should find a comfortable place under the trees to spend the night." Ishihara turned and looked down the road the way they had come. "The camp followers have not caught up yet, but they will. When they are nearby, we must avoid direct contact with them, but their campfires will camouflage our own. Hunter and Steve will have no reason to think we are here."

Jane said nothing. However, the renewed possibility of escaping Wayne and Ishihara gave her a surge of excitement. Later tonight, she would try to get away. For now, lying low suited her just fine.

Harriet spent the evening at Gwenhyvaer's side. After dinner, they joined the other women by a large fireplace in the main hall drinking mead. The palace seemed empty without the men who had gone with Artorius. Only the boys and the elderly men remained. In the tor around them, a skeletal garrison still guarded the walls, but their real protector had ridden out to meet the enemy in his own land.

The other women talked about the Saxons and how long the men would be gone. Harriet noticed that none talked about which ones would not come home. As the fire burned down, the discussion grew quieter, however. Then, one by one, the other women retired for the night to be alone with their thoughts.

"Are you sleepy?" Harriet asked, when she and Gwenhyvaer were left alone in front of the fire.

"A little." Gwenhyvaer shrugged. "But I'm wide awake, too." She gazed into the dwindling flames.

"Shall I put more wood on the fire?"

"No."

Harriet waited in silence, watching her.

"If Artorius doesn't come back, I will be nobody," said Gwenhyvaer quietly.

Harriet wanted to reassure her, to tell her that Artorius would return, but did not dare. A single comforting word might pass as normal, but if Harriet remained in this time for the rest of her life, she would have to learn to keep quiet. The alternative could be gaining, over time, a reputation for knowing the future.

In a superstitious society, knowing the future could make her either a respected wise woman or an evil sorceress, but she would have no control over which one. She would live most comfortably by blending into society, not by standing out. Besides, despite her disbelief in chaos theory, she knew that she really could change the future if she eventually altered the behavior of enough important people.

"If Artorius falls, we are all in trouble," Harriet said carefully. "But he knows his enemy."

"Yes, that's true." Gwenhyvaer brightened a little. "He's been fighting the Saxons for a long time."

Harriet thought again of how young Gwenhyvaer seemed. She reminded herself once more that Gwenhyvaer was a grown woman in this society and almost past her prime marriage years. For that reason, Gwenhyvaer had good reason to be concerned about her future with Artorius.

A woman's position in this society depended largely on the prestige of her father and her husband. Even worse, the status of men in this time was fluid and uncertain, leaving any particular woman with few good choices. The wealth and social strata of Roman society were gone and the social system of medieval England lay many centuries in the future.

Gwenhyvaer knew that if she did not marry well before long, she might have to choose between spending her life as a glorified servant in the palace or marrying a man who rode with Artorius in summer and tended sheep the rest of the year.

"Did your husband ever fight in a war before?" Gwenhyvaer asked. "Did you worry about him all the time?"

"He never fought in a war," said Harriet.

"Really? He's so big. He would make a good warrior. Why didn't he?"

Harriet suppressed a smile, thinking of the First Law. She also realized she would have to embellish the story of her life with Hunter a little in order to answer. "When the Saxons drove us out of Linnuis, on the coast, we had no army left in the area to join. And if he had gone to find Artorius farther inland, I would have been abandoned."

"I see," said Gwenhyvaer. "That's when he took you with him to Gaul."

"That's right."

"I hope I get married soon." Gwenhyvaer turned from the fire to Harriet. "Did you get married young?"

"Well . . . yes."

"How old are you?"

"I'm forty."

Gwenhyvaer straightened in surprise, her eyes wide. "What? Are you joking with me?"

"No. I'm not joking." Harriet smiled at her surprise, knowing that the average life expectancy here was in the early forties, due to the stresses of physical labor, limited diet, and the lack of medical knowledge and dental care. "I'm forty years old."

"But . . . you have *all* your teeth." Gwenhyvaer looked at her mouth again, making sure.

Harriet laughed lightly. "Yes, I do." She shrugged. "I've been fortunate."

"But you just don't look that old. I thought you were . . . oh, I don't know." Gwenhyvaer stared at her face.

Harriet knew that a few individuals lived into their sixties and seventies even in this century, but Gwenhyvaer had good reason to be shocked. Most of the women Harriet's age in this time did look much older. The women she resembled most were closer to thirty.

"Can you . . . I mean, when I get older, can you help me look that way?"

"I don't have any secrets. If I did, I would be glad to share them. But I don't."

Gwenhyvaer nodded slowly and turned to gaze into the fire again.

Long after dark, Jane lay under the stars wrapped up in her blanket. She knew from Wayne's slow, rhythmic breathing that he had fallen asleep. Of course, Ishihara remained alert. She hoped that because she had made no move to escape, he had not focused his attention on her.

She knew that if she prepared herself to make a move, perhaps by taking several deep breaths and shifting her position, Ishihara would hear the difference. That would cost her any element of surprise. Her best chance was to move impulsively, so she did.

All at once, she flung off the blankets, scrambled up, and ran in the faint moonlight toward the camp.

"Hunter!" She screamed as loud as she could. "It's Jane! *Hunter!* Here!"

Footsteps, certainly Ishihara's, sounded behind her, gaining fast.

"Hunter!"

"Hey! Get her!" Wayne yelled sleepily.

Before she could shout again, she stumbled on the uneven sod, losing speed. Ishihara's footsteps come right up behind her and she felt a firm hand grasp her arm.

Ahead of her in the camp, startled voices spoke in puzzled tones, probably sentries.

In another moment, Ishihara slipped one arm around her waist and lifted her off the ground. He moved his other hand from her arm to cover her mouth with his hand. Jane squirmed, trying to shout for Hunter again.

"I know I am not harming you," Ishihara said quietly. "I can feel on my hand that you are breathing sufficiently through your nose."

Jane decided to save her strength and quit fighting. Hunter should have heard her. Now she could only wait.

Hunter was lying on the ground pretending to sleep when he heard Jane's first shout. He recognized her voice even before she identified herself. Instantly he rose and ran through the camp toward the sound, leaving Steve asleep; he did not want to endanger Steve by having him follow. By altering his vision to maximum light receptivity, he saw clearly enough in the moonlight to avoid stumbling over sleeping men or gear.

"You there! Stop!" A man standing on the edge of the camp to Hunter's left shouted, holding up a spear. "Stop, I say! Now!"

Hunter angled his run away from the man, hoping to elude him. However, the man who had shouted began running toward him, as did other sentries on Hunter's right. He changed his angle again, still running toward Jane's voice. Having the sentries follow him might actually help him rescue her.

"Halt! What's wrong with you? Stop!"

Up ahead, Hunter heard hoofbeats canter away. Even at his best robotic running speed, he doubted he could catch the mount. Still, he would normally have tracked the animal through the darkness on the assumption that it carried Jane and probably Wayne.

However, he could not reveal his true running ability to the sentries chasing him. For now, he would have to give up the chase. He came to a halt and turned to face them.

The first sentry ran up to him holding his spear forward. "When I order you to halt, you halt! What is your business out here?"

Five other sentries jogged up behind him, three from one side and two from another. They surrounded Hunter. No one else spoke.

"You must have heard the woman shouting," Hunter said calmly. "I came to help."

"You know her?"

Hunter decided that admitting he knew Jane could endanger her. He did not want the sentries to pay any independent attention to her if they came across her later. "No. I just came to help."

"She's just some camp follower quarreling with a scavenger," said the sentry. "That's their own business, not ours. Stay out of it."

"He's been a troublemaker all day," growled

another man. "I remember him by his height. He almost started a brawl by the wagons this afternoon."

"Is he the one? I heard about that," said the first sentry. He lowered his spear point toward Hunter's abdomen, but did not advance. "The Saxons will give you all the fight you want. We have no rule against chasing a camp follower in the middle of the night, but you'll need your rest. Go on back to your squad and I'll forget about it."

Hunter knew that Ishihara still had to be protecting Jane; in fact, he had probably forced her to stop yelling for help. That took away the immediate First Law imperative for Hunter. He nodded to the sentry and began walking through the moonlight back into the camp with the sentries.

The incident had not been a waste. Now he knew that Jane, with Ishihara and presumably Wayne, was with the army. He would have other chances to reach her.

Ishihara jogged through the moonlight away from the camp, carrying Jane by the waist under one arm. He still held one hand over her mouth to stop her from shouting again. Next to him, Wayne rode the mule at a canter.

By the time Ishihara had run back to their campsite carrying Jane, Wayne had already slipped the bridle on the mule and rolled up the blankets he and Jane used. As soon as he had seen Ishihara coming back with Jane, he had mounted up and kicked the mule into a canter, letting Ishihara take the lead.

Now Ishihara, with his hearing turned up to maximum, could hear Hunter giving explanations to the sentries behind them. Because their voices were stationary, Ishihara knew the pursuit had ended for now. Still, he continued to jog parallel to the river, staying just far enough from the trees for Wayne to ride safely without hitting branches in the darkness.

When Ishihara heard one of the sentries discount Jane's call for help as a dispute among camp followers, he knew the sentries were not concerned. After a while, he stopped, signaling for Wayne to rein in. At this distance, he would hear Hunter's footsteps approaching alone if Hunter made another attempt to come close tonight.

Ishihara set Jane on her feet and released her. "Are you well?"

"Not as well as I could be," she said angrily. "I'm real tired of all this. The idea that you aren't harming me is insane."

"I disagree," said Ishihara.

"We have to gag her," said Wayne. "Or else she'll yell again and give away our position."

"The First Law will not allow that," Jane declared firmly. "It will hurt me and interfere with my breathing. If you don't tie my hands, I'll pull it off. And if you tie me, I might suffocate."

"She's playing games with you," said Wayne. "A careful gag won't kill her."

"I agree with her," said Ishihara. "I cannot allow her to be gagged and tied. We will have to stay far enough from the column so that I can clearly hear any one or two sets of footsteps or hoofbeats approaching us long before they come close. If necessary, we will maintain enough distance so that even Hunter cannot hear her shout again."

"We'll be too far to get MC 6, in that case," said

Wayne. "So what's the point of following him at all? Are you telling me just to give up?"

"We are far enough for both of you to get some rest," said Ishihara. "During the night, I will remain alert for further pursuit and I will consider our options."

Steve felt himself shaken awake early in the morning. When he looked up, Bedwyr grinned and handed him a chunk of cold, cooked mutton and a piece of bread. The earliest light of dawn broke as a yellow haze through the gray clouds, angling among the trees along the river.

"It has to last you all day," said Bedwyr. "Eat it at your leisure, but we won't have any more till we return to the new camp tonight." He also gave Steve a small water skin on a leather strap.

While the rest of the camp rose slowly and built up their campfires, Bedwyr roused his scouting patrol to eat their cold breakfast while saddling and bridling their horses and mounting. Only a few minutes after waking, Steve found himself riding out with Hunter, following the other ten men in the patrol.

When everyone else was out of hearing, Hunter quietly told Steve that he had heard Jane call him for help the night before. Hunter related how the sentries had stopped him. However, they now knew that Wayne, Jane, and Ishihara had followed the column somehow.

A light drizzle fell as the patrol moved away from the camp. First they rode along the near side of the river, walking their horses through the trees, going upstream. Then Bedwyr turned and led them across the river. As they rode through the ford, the horses walked into water up to the level of their underbellies. The river was narrow here, though, and in a moment all the riders had crossed.

When they had left the trees on the far side of the river, Steve saw Bedwyr rein in and glance over his shoulder to make sure all his riders had crossed safely. Then the scouts looked in all directions, across more grassy, rolling hills. In the distance to the east, Steve could see the edge of a forest. To his right, far downstream, he saw another patrol also cross the river and leave the trees. That patrol angled away from them, to the southeast.

Bedwyr suddenly kicked his mount into a canter and rode off toward the distant forest. The rest of the patrol followed. Steve continued to ride in the rear, next to Hunter, squinting in the drizzle.

After about half a kilometer, Bedwyr slowed to a walk again. He waved for the patrol to keep moving in the same direction, but stopped and waited for Steve and Hunter to come up. Then, with a big grin, he fell into step next to them.

"I love this open country," said Bedwyr. "We can spot and ride down any Saxon who hikes out of the forest. As soon as we came across the river, we could see at a glance that this area's clear—not that I thought they've had time to advance this far."

"The forest up ahead could be dangerous to us, then?" Hunter asked.

"We'll be careful, all right, when we get there. Even a foul Saxon can hide among the trees or climb up into the branches. I still say we're too far from their territory to meet them yet, but we won't take chances when we reach any forest." Bedwyr shrugged. "Last year, we didn't see any Saxons for several more days after we passed through here."

"You rode this route last summer?" Steve asked. "We're on the same campaign all over again?"

"Oh, yes." Bedwyr frowned, eyeing the cloudy sky

above them. "More Saxons sail across the Channel every year. We don't have similar numbers coming to join us. Every year, we hope to kill enough to drive them back toward the sea again, but the work feels much the same, year after year."

Steve nodded.

"Last year, we found the Saxons waiting for us on the opposite bank of the River Dubglas. Artorius didn't want to attack against their strength across the water, where our horses would lose the force of their charge in walking or swimming. The Saxons were relying on that, of course; they carry eight-foot lances to unhorse us, and in the water they have a better chance. So we moved up and down the bank to get around them, but the Saxons kept stretching their line to block us."

"What did you do?" Hunter asked.

"When we had stretched their line thin enough, we took advantage of our mobility. Artorius led one end of our line on a fast ride doubling back to the center and charged across the river anyway. They didn't have time to mass their men again to meet us, since they're all on foot."

"And the charge worked?" Steve asked.

"Yes. Even through the water. Their line was so thin that they broke easily. After that, the rest of the Saxon line panicked." Bedwyr grinned. "It was easy slaughter after that, I promise you."

"What did you do during the rest of the summer?" Hunter asked. "That battle itself must not have taken long. Did you fight more than one?"

"We fought only one pitched battle against their full numbers," said Bedwyr. "It occurred late in the season. You see, we spent the early part of the summer jockeying for position."

"Even with your advantage in mobility?" Hunter asked. "Artorius could ride in circles around any Saxon army and attack at any time."

"The Saxons come on like waves of the sea," said Bedwyr. "Yes, we can ride around them, but we must be careful about entering battle. Their numbers are so much greater that Artorius dares not fight them recklessly."

"So what did you do?" Steve asked. "Just wait until the right time?"

"We did plenty of waiting, all right, but we didn't just ride around and look at the landscape, either. Our strategy was to attack the Saxons in small groups."

"What do you mean?" Hunter asked. "How can you separate waves of the sea?"

Bedwyr laughed. "They keep coming, but they don't live together in cities the way Romans do. They live in small villages."

"But once you attacked one, didn't they rally their army together?" Steve asked.

"That was their goal," said Bedwyr. "But we stayed in the saddle and rode hard to confuse them."

"What do you mean?" Steve grinned wryly. "I hope you don't mind all these questions, but it's new to us."

"Of course," said Bedwyr. "That's why Artorius wants the green riders mixing with veterans."

"You said you confused them?"

"Oh, yes," said Bedwyr. "Well, sometimes we drew out Saxon bands from their homes and then rode around them to raid and burn down their villages. We attacked small bands before they could join each other, to fight them without their advantage of numbers. Our patrols let themselves be seen in different places to give the impression that our main column could be coming from any direction."

"I understand," said Hunter.

"We spent all summer maneuvering to avoid fighting a massed Saxon horde, but they finally formed and marched on us. I believe they grouped early this year because of it. Now we'll have to meet them in pitched battle without whittling down their numbers slowly first."

"This campaign could be decided early in the season, then," said Hunter.

"It's possible," said Bedwyr. "But first we'll just have to make sure this route is clear for the main column." He steered his mount out to one side and, with a shout, moved into a canter again.

The rest of the patrol, caught off-guard, hurried after him on their way to the forest ahead.

Bedwyr drew up about twenty meters from the edge of the forest, studying the trees and sky just above it. The rest of the patrol gathered around him. Then the veterans fanned out and rode slowly among the trunks. Steve and Hunter followed Bedwyr.

"No birds have been disturbed," Steve quietly.

"I hear no signs of humans in these trees," Hunter whispered, leaning close to Steve. "Of course, I cannot reveal that to them, but you may know you are in no danger from Saxons right here."

Steve grinned.

Bedwyr led the patrol cautiously through the forest. When the patrol became convinced that no Saxons were there to ambush them, they looked carefully for tracks or firepits that would indicate a recent presence. No one found any sign of them, either, but the patrol did not relax.

As the day advanced, the riders ate from their pieces of mutton and bread. The patrol could not trot or canter through the dense forest, so their progress slowed for the rest of the morning. Shortly after midday, Bedwyr turned his mount to face Steve and Hunter.

"Can you find your way back to the main column?" Bedwyr asked.

"I suppose," Steve said in surprise. "You want us to go back?"

"Have we made a mistake of some sort?" Hunter asked. "We must know."

"No, nothing like that." Bedwyr laughed. "You aren't being punished. But it's time to send word back to Artorius that the way is clear this far. Other advance patrols will report, too, and he will decide exactly which way to go. But the column cannot come much farther than this before it will be time to make camp again."

"It seems early to go back," said Steve, glancing up at the sun. "Only half the day is gone."

"By the time you reach him, and the column advances to this spot, the sun will be low enough," said Bedwyr. "I want to see how you two fare on an errand alone."

"We will do it, of course," said Hunter. "We will find the main column."

"Good! We'll patrol a short distance from here for most of the afternoon. If Artorius decides to lead the column another way, then we'll find the rest of you later." Bedwyr reined his horse around and led his other men forward.

"This task will be simple enough," Hunter said quietly, turning his own mount. "We will follow our own tracks back. At some point, I should be able to hear the hoofbeats in the distance."

Steve grinned. "This is a job I could probably do without you, Hunter. But I'm glad I don't have to."

Jane dozed fitfully during the remainder of the night and woke up tired. She had hoped that Hunter would swoop in during the night and rescue her like one of the knights out of the Arthurian legend that would grow out of all this in years to come. Since he had not, she felt discouraged and wondered why he had not responded to her shouting.

Wayne and Jane ate a cold breakfast of bread and mutton, the same as dinner the evening before. Very little remained. Ishihara built a small fire and boiled water from the river in it before allowing them to drink it. Afterward, Wayne and Jane mounted the mule and Ishihara jogged with them.

Though Wayne and Ishihara had not discussed any detailed plans in her hearing, Jane understood that they had certain limitations. They would either have to make an aggressive move to reach MC 6 this evening, or else they would have to get more food. Ishihara would not allow either human to go hungry and she doubted he would risk trying to get food from the column itself. Because they did not have the equipment necessary to hunt or fish, they would either have to turn back or else abandon Emrys's mule and jump through time and space with or without MC 6. Jane hoped she could get Hunter's attention before Ishihara took one of those choices.

The day passed uneventfully. As before, the riders outpaced the baggage train. Ishihara kept the end of the baggage train within his own sight or hearing, but avoided drawing too close. He also stayed clear of the camp followers.

Once the riders had left the baggage train behind, Wayne turned to Ishihara.

"Hunter must have ridden on ahead by now. If MC 6 is in the baggage train, then Hunter can't get him. We might be able to get MC 6 on the march."

"I do not like our chances," said Ishihara, still jogging next to the mule. "I dare not take Jane too close to the camp followers or near the men in the baggage train. Also, I cannot allow you to approach them alone. The wagon crews will consider all of us simply camp followers and may be hostile. They will probably consider us potential thieves."

"Then you think of something," Wayne growled angrily. "This project has to work somehow. And we haven't had many chances to get MC 6 while Hunter is too far away to interfere. Can't we take advantage of this somehow?"

"The only arrangement I can accept is one that keeps you and Jane away from the camp. If I approach MC 6 without you, I will have the force of the Second Law to order him to come with me as long as he believes I am human. I can tell him to follow me unless he detects that I am a robot."

"If he turns up his hearing and actually listens, he'll hear that you don't have a human heartbeat," said Wayne. "If he studies your skin under magnification, he might see your microscopic solar cells. But all that depends on whether or not he bothers. Since he isn't expecting a robot to approach him in this time period, he may not have his sensitivity turned up to the point where he'll notice."

"In any case, I suggest we wait until after the baggage train stops to make camp before we execute our attempt."

Wayne sighed. "Yeah, all right."

Jane decided not to say anything. She wanted to think of as many objections as she could to pressure Ishihara with the Laws of Robotics. Instead of talking spontaneously, she would think up some arguments now and present them when Ishihara was about to go after MC 6.

Late in the afternoon, Jane could see men riding toward the column from different directions, sometimes along small paths or intersecting roads and sometimes overland. Some rode singly or in small groups; others arrived in large troops, lined up in a military column themselves. The new arrivals moved onto the road ahead of the baggage train.

The baggage train finally reached the spot where the rest of the column had stopped to make camp, in a forest just past a wide stretch of open country. Other troops whom Jane had not seen had also arrived at this rendezvous point, making the camp much larger than it had been the night before. Ishihara led Wayne into the forest and stopped where they could see the baggage train through the trees.

"Have you seen Hunter?" Wayne asked quietly.

"Not yet. The visibility is poor, of course, here in the forest." Ishihara helped Jane down.

Wayne dismounted. "That's good. Hunter will have trouble seeing us, too."

"That is true," said Ishihara. "We must decide exactly what our move will be."

Jane knew that the men in the baggage train could hear her clearly enough if she shouted for help again. However, she had no way of knowing where Hunter was, or if he could hear her. He might be so far up the column that her voice would be drowned out by the sounds of men setting up the camp, yelling orders, and by the hoofbeats of hundreds of horses hobbled for the night. Hunter's failure to respond last night worried her. She decided not to anger Wayne any further by another shout unless she really had reason to think Hunter could help.

"All right, Ishihara," Wayne said firmly. "The chance we've waited for is coming up. No more delays. We have to find a way to get MC 6 now."

"Then what will we do with him?" Ishihara asked. "We must plan our approach based on our escape."

"We'll jump a safe distance away—maybe back to the hills near Emrys's hut, early tomorrow morning. I can open up MC 6 and finally start my investigation into what went wrong. As we've discussed during past missions, I can't go back to Mojave Center until I have information that will work to my advantage with the Oversight Committee."

"I understand. We will simply have to apologize to Emrys for losing the mule."

"Yeah. But when we talked about what to do before, you said you could approach MC 6 alone. Go ahead and see if you can find him. We'll wait right here."

"Don't leave us," Jane said quickly.

"Shut up," said Wayne. "She's just trying to interfere with your thinking, Ishihara."

"The camp followers are coming up behind the baggage train again," said Jane. "If you can't take us to the baggage train, you can't risk leaving us here. If those scavengers come toward us, Wayne can't protect us."

"Nonsense," said Wayne. "Why would they bother us? We don't have anything of value. Go on, Ishihara."

"We have the mule," said Jane. "They could ride it or eat it."

"She has a point," said Ishihara. "In addition, she may escape from you."

"Not if you'll tie her. You refused before. How about just tying her to a tree trunk for a few minutes?"

"I cannot. The First Law—"

"All right, all right. I *know* what it says." Wayne paced angrily among the trees. "Then all three of us can go look for him. You can protect us."

"Among all those men? Even a robot could be overwhelmed," said Jane.

"That is true," said Ishihara.

"Then *you* stay here with her," said Wayne impatiently. "I can go find MC 6 on my own, without the mule. Nobody will have any reason to bother me."

"I cannot allow that under the First Law, either," said Ishihara.

"Why not?" Wayne demanded.

"When Hunter approached the baggage train twenty-four hours ago, he was stopped by a group of men willing to commit violence. I cannot allow you to risk that."

"That's true," said Jane. "That's another risk."

"Shut *up*," Wayne repeated. "Ishihara, I instruct you to suggest a plan that you can accept. At this point, even a fairly low chance of success is better than total inaction. Think of something!"

"Maybe there is no safe way to do this," said Jane. "Too much risk is involved, Ishihara. How about a new approach? Talk to Hunter about working together."

"Don't listen to her, Ishihara," said Wayne. "I gave you an instruction."

"I have a plan," said Ishihara.

"Yeah? What is it?" Wayne folded his arms. "This better be good."

"You take Jane in a slow but deliberate ride on the mule away from the camp and the road. If any riders approach you, ride slowly away from them, but do not appear to flee or they may pursue you to find out why. You can outdistance any camp followers who approach you on foot, so they probably will not try. At the slightest sign of danger to you, shout for me and ride back in my direction. I should be able to reach you quickly. If no trouble develops, then keep riding away from the camp. I will catch up to you, with or without MC 6."

"Exactly what are you going to do?"

"I will attempt to solicit MC 6's aid through a ruse. However, my use of the Second Law depends entirely on his belief that I am human. As we discussed, if he detects that I am a robot, he will not only refuse to obey, but he will flee, alerted to our pursuit."

"You can't leave us like that," Jane insisted. "We'll still be in potential danger."

"This will be acceptable," said Ishihara. "In the event of immediate danger, I will use the belt unit to take us away from here."

"You won't have time to set it," said Jane. "If we're riding away from someone and you're running to meet us, we won't have much time."

"I will set it now." Ishihara reached inside his tunic, opened his abdomen, and brought out the unit. He looked around in the distance, then changed the settings. "In the event we have to use it, we will jump only a few hours into the future, after dark, to a spot half a kilometer away. That will be close enough for us to consider future moves."

Jane could not think of any more arguments. Ishihara, after all, made the final interpretation of what he could accept under the First Law. She sighed and looked at Wayne.

"Mount up," said Wayne.

Ishihara waited until Wayne and Jane had ridden twenty meters away from the camp, out of the trees into open country. Because Ishihara could see they were alone there, he felt he could leave them for a short time. He walked through the trees toward the baggage train.

Moving slowly, Ishihara studied the wagons as he approached them. Because Artorius had stopped to make camp in a forested area, the wagons remained lined up on the road or just off of it, where space permitted. Last night, the wagons had bunched together at the rear of the camp, and the wagon crews had mixed together freely. Now the crews were strung out along the road as they unloaded their wagons.

Ishihara saw that he could approach most of the wagons without attracting the attention of the wagonmaster. In fact, because of the trees, visibility was limited for everyone. That, too, would work to Ishihara's advantage.

He considered his story as he searched for MC 6. Finally, he saw MC 6 standing on the ground near a wagon, unharnessing a team of horses. Ishihara walked up to him.

"I need help," Ishihara said to MC 6 in Briton. "Can you help me?"

MC 6 turned and looked at him. He shrugged, gesturing that he could not understand. Then he turned back to the horses he was tending.

Ishihara looked at another man, standing in the wagon moving small kegs around. "I need help. Can you spare this man for a moment?"

"Eh? Who are you?"

"I drove a wagon behind one of the veteran troops. We just arrived in camp."

"You know this man?"

"No."

"Well, we teamsters should stick together. Hey, you." The man waved his arms to get MC 6's attention. "He's a real cooperative little fellow, but no one can figure out what language he understands."

MC 6 glanced up at the man in the wagon.

"Go with him. Help him." The man in the wagon pointed from MC 6 to Ishihara.

MC 6 nodded.

"Thank you." Ishihara nodded to MC 6 and walked away from the wagon. MC 6 walked with him.

Ishihara could only hope that MC 6 would not think to magnify his hearing or sight and examine Ishihara closely.

Hunter had located Artorius at the head of his column with no trouble. Artorius had responded to Hunter's scouting report by choosing to follow Bedwyr's route for the day. Hunter and Steve rode with him at the head of the column to point out the way.

Late in the day, Bedwyr spotted them and led his patrol back to meet the column. He recommended a place to camp and Hunter and Steve rejoined the scouting patrol. The day had remained uneventful for the scouts, as well as for the main column.

As the other riders dismounted and tended their horses, Steve spoke quietly to Hunter from the saddle.

"Before we dismount, can't we do something about our mission? I enjoyed today's ride, but we don't want to keep this up all summer."

"I agree. However, we have earned some greater respect today, and we are considered more a part of the troop now. Perhaps we can approach the baggage train again and complete our task."

"You told me this morning you heard Jane last night. Can we look for her somehow?"

"I doubt that she remains nearby. Wayne and Ishihara almost certainly have kept their distance since she revealed her presence. First I suggest we attempt to reach MC 6 again. Then we will look for a sign of Jane's presence."

"All right. Got any ideas about how to avoid that Gaius again?"

"Yes. In this forest, I expect the wagons will have to stop in a line alone the road. We should ride parallel to the road on horseback, keeping our distance from the baggage train. I will look and listen for Gaius and for MC 6, as well."

"Sounds good to me. Lead the way."

Hunter reined his mount around the road away from the camp, through the trees, ducking under branches. He heard the hoofbeats of Steve's mount following him. Hunter selected a route that would carry them down the line of the column, close enough for him to hear and see the men at the wagons through the trees but far enough to avoid immediate notice by the wagonmaster.

Jane sat behind Wayne on the mule, riding at a walk away from the camp and the road. At first, they did not bother to turn around as they wove through the trees. They did not run across anyone else, nor did anyone behind them show any interest in where they were going.

After a while, Wayne turned the mule so they could look behind them. By this time, the trees hid the camp from view, though they could hear men shouting orders and horses walking. Without a word, Wayne turned and continued riding away.

As they rode Jane looked back over her shoulder several times, but saw no one. If Ishihara was bringing MC 6, the two robots would have to catch up after Wayne decided to stop and wait. She decided not to do anything until she learned whether or not Ishihara succeeded.

Wayne, following Ishihara's plan, kept the mule moving through the forest. He glanced back over his shoulder every so often, but neither of them spoke. In order to avoid riding directly into tree branches, Wayne had to face forward most of the time.

Jane realized that she had an advantage in riding behind him; she could turn her head and look back without Wayne knowing. The motion of Wayne's shoulders when he turned told her when he was looking behind them even if she had already looked back. She turned her head and continued to look back, despite the awkward angle, as they rode.

As the mule plodded on, Jane finally saw a motion through the trees behind them. Ishihara was jogging after them, closely followed by MC 6. The forest was so dense here that they had come close without being seen; on the damp earth, their footsteps had not been loud enough for her to hear.

If Ishihara had induced MC 6 to come with him somehow, instead of grabbing him and bringing him by force, Jane figured that MC 6 had his hearing turned on. That meant she could call to him in English. Suddenly encouraged, she looked for a soft spot on the ground among the trees.

Suddenly Jane slipped off the mule, pretending to lose her balance. She allowed herself to fall on the ground, where she judged she could land safely. Startled, Wayne reined in and looked back at her.

"Ishihara, help me!" Jane shouted. Then, as Ishihara ran toward her, she looked at the other robot. "MC 6, run! They're going to dismantle you!"

The small component robot instantly darted to one side and ran through the trees. He took off at an angle away from both them and the column to their rear. His actions were driven by the Second Law to obey her instruction to run and by the Third Law to protect himself.

"Hey!" Wayne shouted, finally seeing MC 6 for the first time. "Stop! I order you! Stop, robot!" He wheeled the mule around and rode after MC 6, leaning low to avoid tree branches. "Halt! I need you under the First Law!"

MC 6 did not seem to believe that. Jane did not see him come back. He might have turned off his hearing once he understood the danger present to him.

Jane had not been sure her ruse would work; MC 6 might have felt required by the First Law to come forward with Ishihara to help her. However, he had apparently judged that Ishihara would take care of her adequately. She had gambled on that. If she had told MC 6 that she was unharmed, Ishihara would also have been freed of the need to help her and he might have captured MC 6.

Instead, Ishihara now hesitated where he stood. He was momentarily undecided between the immediate need to care for Jane and the First Law issue requiring him to capture MC 6 for Wayne's long-term welfare. Every moment helped MC 6 escape.

"Help me up, Ishihara," said Jane, to stall him further. She remained on the ground.

Ishihara hurried toward her and knelt down. "Are you injured?"

Jane decided that telling extreme lies would be a mistake; teaching him not to trust her could backfire if she was in real trouble. Stalling, on the other hand, seemed safe enough. she said nothing. Behind Ishihara, Wayne came riding back, scowling. MC 6 had escaped him.

"Ishihara! Go get him!" Wayne yelled.

"Are you injured?" Ishihara repeated.

"Not seriously. Please help me up."

"Of course."

"Ishihara, she's faking!" Wayne dismounted near them. "Track that robot now, before he gets back to the wagons! I couldn't ride fast enough in this stupid forest to keep up, but he hasn't gone far."

Jane remained passive as Ishihara put one arm under her shoulders and raised her up. Then he shifted his position and helped her stand. She took a deep breath and leaned on Ishihara's shoulder.

"I'll take care of her!" Wayne yelled. "Ishihara, go *get* him!"

"You seem unharmed," Ishihara said to Jane.

"Yes, I'll be all right."

"Now!" Wayne grabbed Ishihara's arm and pushed after MC 6. "I'll watch her!"

Ishihara finally turned and jogged in the direction MC 6 had gone.

Wayne watched him go.

As soon as Wayne turned away, Jane ducked under a branch and ran.

"Hey!" Wayne yelled behind her. "Oh, no, you don't! Come back here!"

Jane darted around a sapling and bent down to avoid another low-hanging branch, but she felt Wayne grab her hair from behind. He yanked, pulling her head back. She threw her arms around the branch and hung on, but could not move her head.

"Ishihara!" Jane yelled. Then she let out a loud, long, scream, much more exaggerated than the situation really warranted.

"Shut up!" Wayne put his other hand over her mouth and tried to pull her away from the tree branch.

Jane struggled, but she was not really angry or scared. She was still deliberately provoking Wayne and forcing Ishihara to protect her instead of catching MC 6. She bent her knees, dropping to the ground as she thrashed in his grasp. Wayne had to fall, too, in order to hang onto her.

Neither of them spoke. Jane let go of the branch, but tried to pull his hand away from her mouth. In a moment, she heard footsteps running toward them. Then suddenly Wayne released her. She let herself fall back onto the grass, looking up.

Ishihara had pulled Wayne away and now held him firmly as they both stood over her.

"I told you to catch MC 6," Wayne growled, but he did not sound as angry as before.

"You know I cannot allow this," said Ishihara. "If I release you, will you remain calm?"

"Yeah, yeah, all right. But you've been manipulated. She's done it to both of us."

Ishihara let go of him.

"You didn't have to grab me," said Jane, remaining where she lay. "You could have let me go." That, too, was for Ishihara's benefit.

"Are you harmed?" Ishihara asked.

"Not really. But I didn't like it much." She looked at Wayne. "Keep your hands to yourself from now on."

"She's fine," Wayne wearily. "And I'm not going to hurt her. You still might have a chance to get MC 6, if you hurry. You can track him."

"No, you can't," said Jane. "As soon as you leave again, I'm running away. And Wayne will try to stop me again and we'll wind up wrestling around again. Ishihara, you either have to stay here and protect me from Wayne or let me go."

"I won't hurt her," said Wayne. "I've never wanted to hurt her. But we can't let her tell Hunter where we are—or where MC 6 has gone, either."

"You can't trust him," said Jane. "You just saw him grab me and pull me down."

"If you promise not to run away, I can trust him," said Ishihara.

"I refuse to promise," said Jane. "In fact, I promise to run away every chance I get from now on."

"Ishihara, can't you see what she's doing?" Wayne demanded. "This whole argument is set up to stop you from getting MC 6, and that's all it is."

"The First Law has no exceptions," said Ishihara. "I must make my own interpretation of priorities. Unless you decide to let Jane go find Hunter on her own, I must remain with both of you."

Wayne sighed with resignation. "I can't do that. We might as well give up as do that."

"Then I suggest we move somewhat farther from the camp and make our own camp for the night," said Ishihara. "The sun will go down soon."

"All right," said Wayne. "But if you're staying here instead of chasing MC 6, make sure that she stays, too."

Jane indulged in an impish grin, relieved that she had foiled the capture of MC 6. "Why, of course, Wayne. Anything you want."

Steve rode up and down a route roughly parallel to the road with Hunter. Neither of them spoke. Steve could hear the men and horses of the baggage train and occasionally saw them through the trees.

Finally Hunter reined in and turned to Steve.

"I have heard and seen no sign of MC 6. While I grant that he may not be speaking, I should be able to hear his footsteps, which are of a distinctively light weight among grown men. If he was helping others, I should hear them talk about him as they work, if they do not address him directly."

"You think he figured out that we came from his time to get him?"

"I must consider it possible. He may have studied my skin with magnified vision while we spoke with Gaius last night. Also, he may have been approached by Wayne and Ishihara, in which case they could have revealed their purpose."

"I guess if you'd heard any sign of them, you would have told me."

"I have not. As we discussed before, I expect that after Jane shouted for my help, Wayne and Ishihara took her a safe distance away from the column."

"If they know MC 6 came with the column, they must have followed. Let's go look for tracks."

Hunter looked through the trees at the position of the sun. "I do not estimate we have enough light to pursue any tracks for long."

"Wait a minute. Didn't you say a while ago that if we couldn't find MC 6, we could look for Jane?"

"We have taken more time than I expected in searching for MC 6. I cannot allow you to miss dinner. Nor can we wander too far from the camp before darkness falls."

"I can miss a meal if I have to. Besides, we don't have to be gone long. Let's look around."

"Agreed."

Hunter rode back up the route they had taken before, but now he examined the ground. Steve said nothing. He felt trapped by their need to perform duties in the column.

"Here." Hunter stopped and pointed to hoofprints, accompanied by smaller depressions in the grass and soft earth.

"You found him?"

"I have found the tracks of one mount and the footsteps of Ishihara and another set of the right size to be MC 6." Hunter looked through the trees away from the road. "I surmise that Wayne and Jane rode double on the animal."

"You mean they got him?"

"I see that they have him, but only since the baggage train halted. Wayne has not had time to dismantle MC 6 yet."

"Let's go!"

"No," said Hunter. "I will go. I suggest you return to the squad and tell Bedwyr that a personal matter arose for me. Assure him that I will not need dinner and that I will return in time to do my duties tomorrow."

"He'll expect you to come back in time to get a night's sleep. I can't tell him you don't need it."

"Listen carefully for my voice. If I call you from the camp, it will mean we are ready to leave the column permanently. Otherwise, I will simply return during the night to resume my position."

"I should go with you. Maybe I can help."

"We must maintain our goodwill with Bedwyr."

"Yeah, all right. Good luck. Get going." Steve kicked his mount and rode up the line, hoping that Hunter would get MC 6 quickly.

Hunter leaned low and rode at a quick walk, dodging trees. The tracks in the soft earth were clear and fresh. This was the best opportunity to get both MC 6 and Jane that he had yet seen.

When Hunter reached a spot where the grass and some small bushes had been crushed, he studied the tracks and the marks carefully. He saw that MC 6 had run away from this spot alone, without reaching the area where the ground cover had been disturbed. He guessed that Jane had somehow freed MC 6, though he could not tell how.

Because the hoofprints and Ishihara's tracks led in a different direction from those of MC 6, Hunter had to decide which way to go.

Jane had apparently remained in Isihara's company, so Hunter judged that finding MC 6 was more urgent. He decided to track MC 6 as long as the waning daylight held out. As he did so, he observed that the component robot did not make any effort to hide his tracks, probably relying on speed and agility to avoid human pursuit.

The forest darkened quickly, however, and Hunter realized that he could not continue tracking MC 6 for long. Even if he used the maximum light receptivity of his vision, too much of the moonlight would be blocked by the canopy of leaves overhead for him to see fine details. For now, his infrared vision could still perceive the faint warm spots on the ground left by MC 6's feet, but the heat was dissipating quickly. Hunter would not catch MC 6 before it vanished.

He saw no point in riding on. However, before he returned to the camp, he reviewed MC 6's route in hope of finding a pattern. The component robot seemed to be moving roughly parallel to the road, going ahead of the main column in anticipation of its journey tomorrow.

Hunter guessed that MC 6 still hoped to prevent the violence of the coming battle, as unlikely as that seemed. Since Wayne and Ishihara had located him in the baggage train, Hunter felt certain that MC 6 would not return there. Still, Hunter might be able to pick up his trail tomorrow.

He turned and rode back to the camp.

As Steve ate bread and mutton again by the patrol's campfire, he noted that Bedwyr kept glancing into the gathering darkness. Bedwyr had not objected to Hunter pursuing a personal errand, but he seemed uncomfortable. When Hunter finally arrived, however, Bedwyr simply offered him his dinner.

During a walk to the latrine, Steve asked Hunter what he had found. Hunter explained and Steve resigned himself to another wait. During the evening, Steve hoped Jane would yell for help again, but if she did, even Hunter did not hear her.

As Steve lay rolled in his blanket near the dwindling campfire, he felt trapped again by their presence in the column. At this point, Hunter knew both Jane and MC 6 to be nearby but not actually traveling in the column. Tomorrow, Steve and Hunter would have to ride out with the patrol instead of searching for either of them; in the meantime, Ishihara would probably start tracking MC 6 in earnest.

Steve wondered, as he drifted off to sleep, if Hunter would consider deserting tomorrow. He would ask when he got Hunter alone. Then, tired from the long day in the saddle, he slept soundly.

A hand on his shoulder shook him awake.

Steve rolled over, blinking groggily. The night was still black. He heard other men in the squad stirring. By the faint glow of the embers nearby, he saw a man's shadow standing over him.

"We must ride," Bedwyr said grimly. "Move fast." He walked away and bent over someone else.

Steve forced himself up. He could feel that he had only slept a few hours at most. His eyes adjusted to the faint moonlight and he saw that Hunter had already brought their horses up.

Sleepily Steve rose and slid his sword into his belt. He stumbled to his saddle where it lay on the ground. As he threw it on his mount he spoke quietly, his voice rough with sleep.

"Have you heard what's going on?"

"Yes," said Hunter. "More patrols rode out at sundown. They knew they would have to ride slowly in the moonlight and they expected to camp alone for the night at a forward position, then report back in the morning. Instead, before stopping to make camp, one of them stumbled across the campfires of the entire Saxon army. The riders just got back a few minutes ago."

"That's right," said Bedwyr, holding out more bread and cold mutton for them. "The Saxons have already crossed the River Dubglas and marched out to meet us on our own territory this year."

Steve accepted his breakfast and slipped both pieces into his tunic. He glanced up and down the dark camp. "No one else is up yet?"

"No need to disturb them," said Bedwyr. "On foot, the Saxons will need a full day's march or more to reach us. At dawn, Artorius will lead the column forward with a good night's sleep. Over four thousand of our veterans met us on this site yesterday. In daylight, the column will cover the distance in less than four hours. By midday, he will draw close enough to the Saxons to view the terrain and choose his tactics."

"What is our assignment?" Hunter asked.

"We will reach them by dawn or shortly after, riding slowly in the moonlight," said Bedwyr. "When we have seen which way they march in the morning, we will report back to Artorius so he knows where to find them."

Hunter nodded.

Steve swung up into his saddle. Hunter gave him his spear and shield. Within minutes, the rest of the patrol had also mounted. Bedwyr led them out of camp at a walk, riding single file among the other squads and the trees.

At first, Steve was excited by the danger of their new task. However, they all knew that the real danger lay several hours away at the earliest. Steve's enthusiasm waned quickly. Throughout the remaining hours of darkness, the patrol continued at a walk, remaining in single file so that only Bedwyr, in the lead, had to find a path.

When enough light appeared in the east to see into the distance, Bedwyr halted for a moment, looking around in all directions. Steve did the same, but they were still in a forest; he saw nothing but trees. Then, without a word, Bedwyr led them forward again.

Hunter rode with his aural sensitivity at maximum. At midmorning, he heard ten pairs of human footsteps in the forest ahead before any of the humans in the patrol reacted. However, a moment later, several small birds fluttered out of the trees ahead. Bedwyr stopped immediately, raising one hand, palm open, to halt the entire patrol.

Hunter felt his own tension rising under the First Law. On the surface, the First Law required him to stop the violence entirely. He knew he could not, of course, without altering history.

However, Hunter would protect Steve. As a last resort, Hunter would even return them to their own time, though he hoped to avoid that. He reached inside his tunic to make sure that its folds did not interfere with his access to the belt unit hidden inside his abdomen and to set the time at which they would return if necessary. Satisfied, he listened carefully to the movement of the unseen men ahead.

Bedwyr hefted his spear and rode forward slowly. Now the other riders fanned out, moving to surround the area where the birds had been disturbed. Hunter allowed the riders in front of him to open some distance before he followed them. Steve remained behind him.

The movement of horses sent another flight of birds out of the branches overhead. Hunter heard shouts from the forest in front of them; in response, Bedwyr leaned low and kicked his mount into a trot. The other riders in the patrol did the same, whooping and yelling.

Hunter heard bowstrings plucked as he moved forward slowly. Steve came up alongside him, looking around uneasily. The rest of the patrol soon rode out of sight among the trees. Hunter turned to Steve.

"Remain behind me. We will pretend that the trees have blocked our charge." He rode forward at a trot, too, on Bedwyr's path.

More shouts and the sound of metal clanging reached Hunter before he could see the skirmish. He rode between two large trees and saw two strange men lying dead on the ground under the trees. Next to them, one of Bedwyr's men lay on his back with two arrows in his torso.

Hunter heard the sounds of men running away on foot and hoofbeats following them. No one else was in sight yet. The patrol was dispersing as the riders' pursuit took them in different directions.

"You okay?" Steve asked. "With people getting killed around you?"

"Yes," said Hunter. "From all our missions, I have learned to focus on my larger task in these situations. I feel great stress, however."

"You want to take off?" Steve asked. "We could claim to get lost."

"Not yet, but soon. For now, we should stay close to Bedwyr and find out what he will do next."

"Lead on."

In a few minutes, Hunter and Steve caught up to Bedwyr, who had stopped at the edge of a clearing.

Bedwyr glanced back and grinned at them over his shoulder. "Come up and see."

Hunter drew up next to him and looked down a long, open, grassy slope. At its base, over a kilometer away, an army of men carrying long lances and shields, wearing short swords, marched at an angle. Apparently they hoped to circle around the slope rather than climb it. They did not march in formation, but in a long, formless line, its far end hidden by another forest on the far side of the downward slope.

"What are you smiling about?" Steve asked. "They've massed their numbers, as you said. They'll be harder to defeat this way, won't they?"

"Too late to worry about that," said Bedwyr. "But we found them before they found us. That's our task. Now, then. Artorius will have marched at dawn. I estimate that leaves him four hours' ride behind us. Can you find the column again, as you did yesterday?"

"Yes, I believe so," said Hunter.

"Good. I will send both of you; I want you both to gain more experience. If you ride directly toward Artorius as he continues to advance, you should meet him in only two hours. Even if you have a little trouble locating him, you will not need much more time."

"What is our message?"

"Tell Artorius where we have found the Saxons and which way they are marching. In another hour, I will send more couriers back to report whether their line of march has changed or remained the same. In the meantime, I will rally the patrol. From a safe distance, we will watch the Saxons march and fall back to remain clear of them."

"Very well," said Hunter.

"Go now. Good luck."

Hunter wheeled his mount and started back through the trees, with Steve riding beside him. When they had ridden out of Bedwyr's hearing, Hunter spoke quietly again. "This is excellent for our purposes. After we report to the Dux, we can ride forward again, ostensibly to rejoin Bedwyr. Instead, we can pursue our own agenda."

"You mean track MC 6," said Steve. "It sounds perfect to me."

Hunter had no trouble locating Artorius, as the column followed the winding road through the forest. The ride was as uneventful as the return ride the previous day had been. Hunter and Steve fell into step with Artorius on the march and Hunter reported quickly.

"Well done," said Artorius. He wore the same plain steel cap and leather armor as his men. "I expect the Saxons are marching overland to reach this very road. When they reach it, they hope it will lead straight to the heart of our land—which it would, if we were not here to meet them."

Hunter said nothing, waiting.

Artorius smiled grimly, looking up the road. "Well, then. We will march forward for another hour, until the next couriers from Bedwyr arrive to tell us if I am right. In the meantime, we will watch for open country, where we can use our mobility to the greatest advantage. When we know for certain where to find the Saxons, we will prepare a welcome for them."

"May we have leave to rejoin our patrol?" Hunter asked politely.

"I have a message for you to take," said Artorius. "You will precede us only by a short distance now. By the time you find them again, they will have fallen back almost to the point where we are likely to meet. Since you can take the road for the first part of this route, you will move faster than you did riding overland through the forest. Tell Bedwyr to select a good battle site if he can. He will know what to look for—open country with high ground for us."

"Very well," said Hunter.

"Go now."

Hunter kicked his mount, leading Steve up the road at a canter.

When they had left the column behind, Steve called out to Hunter. "Does this mean we can't look for Jane or MC 6 now, after all?"

"First we must give the message to Bedwyr," said Hunter. "He must receive this instruction."

"It doesn't sound that important. Won't Bedwyr know to look for a good battleground? He knows what he's doing."

"I expect so, but I cannot take the chance," said Hunter. "If we had not come back to this time, he would have sent other messengers to report to Artorius. We must assume that they would have obeyed Artorius's order to give this message to Bedwyr. I cannot risk failing the instruction."

"This is ridiculous," said Steve. "We aren't getting anywhere."

Together, they cantered on up the road.

Ishihara led Wayne and Jane on MC 6's trail all morning. From what Ishihara could tell by the freshness of the tracks, they were not catching up; the small component robot could move faster through the dense forest than the mule and its riders. However, Ishihara did see that MC 6 continued to stay near the road, zigzagging through the trees near it. Finally Ishihara quit pursuing MC 6 through the trees and simply moved up along the side of the road. They moved parallel to the head of the column.

"MC 6 has some purpose regarding the army," said Ishihara. "We do not need to follow his tracks. Sooner or later, he will return to the road somewhere in front of us."

"He wants to stop the coming battle," said Wayne. "As hopeless as any attempt by him will be. At some point, probably soon, I think he will approach Artorius and ask him to negotiate peace with his enemy."

"I do not see how," said Ishihara. "A man at the wagons told me he does not seem to have learned to speak the local language. MC 6 has only communicated with gestures."

"Maybe he's listening carefully and learning on the sly," said Wayne.

Jane, again riding behind Wayne, said nothing. She had remained silent all morning.

"How do you feel?" Ishihara asked.

"I'm fine," said Wayne.

"I'm starved," said Jane. "Since we ate the last of our food last night, you know we can't go on indefinitely. If I go much longer without food, you know I'll be harmed."

"Don't pay any attention," said Wayne. "She can go without a meal or two, just like I can. Let's get MC 6 today and then worry about it."

"Agreed," said Ishihara. He knew Jane had a point, but they were close to MC 6 and Hunter did not seem to be nearby. Ishihara expected to find MC 6 soon. For now, he led them forward, keeping track of the head of the column.

Early in the afternoon, a clear sound of jogging footsteps reached Ishihara from the road in front of the column. Ishihara signaled for Wayne to halt and slipped quietly through the trees so that he could see the road.

MC 6 stood in the center of the muddy road, holding out his arms. Several of the men riding with Artorius shouted for him to stand aside. The small robot did not move, however, and finally Artorius himself raised his hand for the column to halt, and reined in.

"Who are you, fellow? Do you have news of the Saxons?" Artorius looked at MC 6 sternly but not angrily.

MC 6 responded in the same language; Ishihara guessed that he must have learned it the same way Ishihara had. "Many people will die and many more will be injured in the coming war. Please avoid the violence. Speak with your enemies and search for agreements. You need not fight with them."

"The man is crazed," a man next to Artorius said quietly. "At night, he may howl at the moon."

"Perhaps he has been touched by the gods," Artorius answered softly. Then he raised his voice. "Have you any news, friend? Any word that the Saxons seek peace?"

"No," said MC 6. "But if you make the first offer, they might listen."

"I fear not, my friend," said Artorius. He sounded resigned rather than hostile. "If they did not wish to fight, they would not keep coming across the Channel to take what we have. And if we do not stop them here, they will kill us and our families." Artorius signaled for the column to advance. "Stand aside, friend."

MC 6 obeyed, but he called out to Artorius again to parley with the enemy. Artorius ignored him as he rode past. MC 6 jogged alongside, still speaking to him, but no one listened to him now. Finally, MC 6 turned and slipped into the forest again, far up the road.

Ishihara understood that MC 6's effort was naive and simplistic. As a robot himself, however, he also knew that the First Law did not offer any advice on how to prevent a war. It only dictated that a robot must not allow harm to humans, leaving the means up to the individual robot.

If Hunter's team and Wayne and Ishihara did not interfere with MC 6, he would eventually try again to prevent violence. If no one stopped him, he might eventually gain the trust of Artorius or a Saxon leader, and actually succeed in lessening the destruction. He just had not had time yet to work out a way to accomplish this. Ishihara saw more clearly than ever that to preserve their own time, they could not allow him to remain here.

A shift in the hoofbeats of the column got his attention. When he looked, he realized that orders had been given for different troops of riders to leave the road and fan out to each side. Ishihara suspected that the Saxon army had been located nearby.

He waved for Wayne to ride up behind him. As the riders changed formation, MC 6 would be unnoticed in the confusion. It would be a good time to catch him unaware and distracted. However, they would have to avoid the riders themselves while they tried to catch the robot.

Steve and Hunter rode back to Bedwyr with their message. They found Bedwyr's patrol waiting for both the Saxons and Artorius at the far edge of a large, wide clearing. It did not have much of a slope in any direction, but no trees would block the charge of Artorius's riders. The road ran right through the middle of the clearing.

Soon after Steve and Hunter arrived, they caught the first glimpses of Artorius's riders at the edge of the clearing behind them. However, they no longer rode up the road in a column. Instead, they had already taken positions in the trees and now waited for the Saxons to advance into the clearing.

"I was right," Steve muttered. "Bedwyr picked a battle site on his own. He didn't need the message we brought from Artorius."

"The fact remains that we fulfilled our historical role," Hunter whispered back.

Another rider in the patrol trotted out of the trees ahead of them and stopped next to Bedwyr. They spoke too quietly for Steve to hear. Then Bedwyr turned and waved for his patrol to pull back. To their rear, a man next to Artorius waved for them to come.

Steve and Hunter followed him at a trot across the clearing. The patrol halted at the trees where Artorius's riders stood waiting. From here, Steve saw that the trees were filled with riders.

"Good work, Bedwyr," said Artorius. "As always. I want you and your men to ride from here as we charge."

"We are honored," said Bedwyr.

The other riders around Artorius made room for the patrol. Bedwyr and his men turned their horses and waited, also. Ahead of them, the clearing remained empty. However, birds fluttered out of the trees beyond it,

"This clearing isn't very big," said Steve quietly. "Only the front of the enemy line can be trapped here."

"It's the biggest open area in the vicinity," said Bedwyr, with a shrug. "It will do."

"Can't they hear the horses? Or don't they have patrols that have seen us?" Steve asked. "They must know we're here."

"They have seen our patrol, and others, from time to time today," said Bedwyr. "But they can't know exactly where Artorius will meet them. With our advantage in mobility, we don't have to find an ideal battleground. If we panic the front of their line, the others will be thrown into confusion. Then we can ride them down."

Steve said nothing else. After all, according to Harriet's history, Artorius had succeeded. These guys knew what they were doing.

"The task never seems to end," said Artorius.

Bedwyr looked at him.

"We have often said, Bedwyr, that the Saxons come on like waves of the sea. Every year we defeat them, yet the next year we face more of them than ever."

"You have never lost a battle to them," said Bedwyr. "You're the kind of leader bards sing about."

Artorius gazed grimly into the distance. "I wonder. Bards sing about great victories, not those who fight forever with no success. I wonder if anyone will ever remember our names."

Steve smiled but did not dare answer.

Hunter heard the advancing march of thousands of Saxon feet while the Britons around him still spoke quietly among themselves, unaware of their enemy. The coming battle caused Hunter's tension under the First Law to rise, but he focused his attention on Steve. When the charge began, they would have to ride forward with the riders or risk colliding with those behind them. However, as soon as they could lose themselves in the confusion of battle, Hunter would take Steve off to one side. Their search for MC 6 and Jane could begin in earnest.

The men around Hunter stiffened suddenly. Ahead of them, the Saxons came tramping down the road, out of the forest. They, too, looked around warily, aware that their enemy lay near.

Suddenly a rider right behind Artorius raised an old, dented Roman post horn and blew an alarm. As the riders whooped and charged up the road, leveling their spears, Hunter and Steve kicked their mounts and rode with them. Ahead of them, the Saxons in the front swung their long lances down to a horizontal position or hefted their spears and threw them. Then they braced themselves for the impact. Arrows flew from the ranks behind them.

Hunter allowed his mount to canter forward, but reined in to keep his speed down. Next to him, Steve did the same, leaning low to avoid arrows and spears; riders behind them rushed past, shouting and screaming. Then, up ahead, the clash of men, horses, and weapons reached Hunter. On each side of the road, riders charged across the clearing and into the trees, then turned toward the road to catch the marching Saxons on the flanks.

"Follow me!" Hunter shouted to Steve. He angled to one side, and Steve rode after him away from the road. None of the riders paid particular attention to them; now that the battle had been joined, the riders in the rear ranks were picking their way among the trees to find a route to the action.

Hunter led Steve out to the far left flank of riders, then entered the trees. The sounds of fighting were clear, but the men and horses were out of sight. Steve rode up next to him and they stopped.

A quick motion in the trees ahead caught Hunter's attention.

"*Now* can we look for MC 6?" Steve demanded. "It's now or never, isn't it?"

"No need to look," said Hunter, pointing forward through the trees. "I glimpsed him over here a moment ago. There he is. Come on!"

Hunter kicked his mount and bent down low under the branches. MC 6 jogged through the trees toward a group of five Saxons, who turned at the sound of hoofbeats to defend themselves. Hunter judged that MC 6 still hoped to prevent harm to some of the humans somehow. Steve circled away from them, on a path to drive MC 6 back toward Hunter.

The Saxon warriors also dodged away from him. Instead of fleeing, however, they ran toward Hunter, fanning out among the trees so that the trunks protected them. Hunter just wanted to ride by them after MC 6, but he had no chance. Two spears came flying at him at once; he caught one on his shield and twisted in the saddle a second later to avoid the second.

A third Saxon threw a spear. While Hunter knocked it away with his shield, the first two Saxons ran toward him with their short swords raised.

Hunter swung his spear in a low arc, knocking their sword blades aside; they were startled to see him ride past them instead of pausing to fight.

MC 6 had darted away from Steve and came running up behind the Saxons.

"Stop! Stop fighting!" MC 6 called out. "You must not hurt each other!"

"Don't move," Steve shouted. "Under the Second Law, I order you to stop and join me! A First Law imperative requires that you cooperate long enough to hear me explain."

As Hunter dodged two more Saxons running alongside him, slashing at his legs, he saw MC 6 turn and run to Steve. The danger of battle and his plan to communicate with humans had forced MC 6 to keep his hearing turned on. Past them, Hunter also spotted Ishihara running toward them. In a tree branch behind Ishihara, Wayne and Jane sat together about four meters above the ground, over a mule.

"Steve!" Hunter shouted as he raised his shield and swung his spear back and forth to block the sword-strokes of his attackers. "Ishihara is behind you!" Hunter tried to ride forward again, but one of the Saxons had grabbed his bridle, holding his mount. Hunter could not advance without harming the Saxons.

"Come on!" Steve yelled to MC 6. He dropped his spear so he could reach down with one arm to help the robot mount. "Swing up here!"

Hunter defended himself from the Saxons as they tried to pull him off his horse. He backed his mount away from them and flung his spear in front of a Saxon, to make him back away. Then he drew his sword and blocked the swords of the remaining Saxons.

Because Hunter still carried the team's belt unit, Steve could not take MC 6 home on the spot. Besides, Hunter could not trigger it until Steve and MC 6 were much closer to him and their horses and the Saxons were out of range of the unit. Hunter heard other riders coming toward them now; he hoped they would drive the Saxons back.

Ishihara had stopped about ten meters away when MC 6 mounted behind Steve. Hunter guessed that Ishihara's need to protect Wayne and Jane on the edge of the battle had interfered with his instructions to get MC 6, especially now that Steve already had him.

"Get him!" Wayne yelled. "Ishihara, get MC 6!"

Steve finally turned and saw Ishihara. "Stay away! Back off!" Then he turned and rode toward Hunter.

Ishihara remained where he was. Other riders appeared out of the trees, shouting as they leaned low under tree branches. They rode toward Hunter.

"Not too close!" Hunter called to Steve as he continued to fight the Saxons around him defensively.

Hunter swung his shield outward, pushing back one of the men on his left. At the same moment, he blocked the sword of a man on his right. He saw a spear coming toward him from a third Saxon also on his left and ducked to his right, but the motions of his arms were already committed and the momentum prevented him from avoiding the spear.

The heavy spear smashed into his left shoulder and he instantly felt a loss of control over his shoulder and arm. His energy level also dropped suddenly as some of his electrical circuits were severed. Though his awareness level did not change, he could no longer raise his shield. He felt the Saxons grab his limp left arm and pull. Afraid that some of his internal robotic parts would become exposed to them if he resisted, he allowed himself to be dragged off his mount to the ground.

Steve stopped several yards from Hunter with MC 6, confident that Hunter would fight his way free of the Saxons and join him.

"Get down and stay with me," Steve ordered MC 6. As soon as the component robot had jumped to the ground, Steve dismounted. Then he looked up and saw Hunter wrenched from his horse by two Saxons. One of them raised his sword to slash at Hunter; Steve drew his sword and cocked his arm to throw it. "Hey! Hey, you!"

"No." MC 6 grabbed his arm and held it fast. "Do not harm anyone."

Suddenly, before the Saxons struck Hunter, they saw the other riders bearing down on them. The Saxons broke and ran as the riders closed in behind them.

Steve waited until Hunter had been left alone. Then he stuck his sword back into his belt and ran to Hunter. "Come on!"

MC 6 followed.

In another moment, the riders had moved out of sight. Shouts and the clash of weapons resounded through the trees nearby, but the movement of the battle had shifted the lines away from them. Suddenly Steve found himself with MC 6 and Hunter damaged on the ground in front of him.

"Hunter, can you hear me? Can I pull out the spear? Or will that make it worse?"

"Pull it out straight, please," Hunter said calmly.

"Ishihara! Get back here," Wayne called. He stood a distance away through some trees, near the mule. Jane and Wayne remained on a tree branch above them.

Steve took the spear shaft in his hands but looked back over his shoulder. "Jane! Come on!"

"I'm coming!" She jumped off the branch suddenly, dodging Wayne's arm as he grabbed for her. However, as she tried to run toward Steve and Hunter, Ishihara blocked her way. She could not possibly beat his robotic reflexes and speed. In a moment, Ishihara had taken her arm, and he began to pull her back toward the mule.

Steve almost let go of the spear shaft to run to her, but realized that he could not help right now. If he approached Ishihara with MC 6, then Ishihara would try to grab the component robot and might succeed; he still followed Wayne's orders under the Second Law. Steve also feared that if he left MC 6 with Hunter and ran to help Jane, Ishihara would dodge around Steve and would either catch MC 6 or at least chase him away. Then Steve would have to start over again—maybe without Hunter's help.

Steve decided he would have to get Jane away from Wayne later. He drew the spear out slowly, as straight as he could. Then he knelt and unlaced Hunter's leather armor. He loosened it enough to fumble in Hunter's clothes for the torso panel that hid the belt unit.

Another glance over his shoulder told him that Wayne and Ishihara had taken Jane out of sight. Their mule's hoofbeats had been camouflaged by the sounds of battle. Those sounds had grown more distant as Artorius's riders drove the Saxons back.

"Here's the deal, Hunter," said Steve. "I'll get the belt unit out and take us all back to our own time. We can secure MC 6, get you repaired, and then come back just a minute after we left to rescue Jane."

"No." Hunter took Steve's wrist in his other hand and stopped him. "Listen carefully. I have identified a new problem. I have been running my self-diagnostic programs and I cannot be returned to our time in this condition."

"Why not? You're a robot—it's not like moving an injured human. Even if we do a little more damage moving you, we can still get you repaired."

"That is not what I mean," said Hunter. "The trauma damage has triggered a more critical problem, according to the monitors that study my functions on a microscopic level. My system will explode with nuclear force if I return to our own time this way."

"What? That doesn't make any sense." Realizing that they could not leave before talking this out, Steve drew his hand away and glanced around.

No one remained in sight. MC 6 stood motionless over Hunter and Steve. For the moment, they could talk safely.

"I don't get it, Hunter," said Steve. "You said the instability in the atoms of the component robots resulted from the particle shower in the time travel sphere, which combined the miniaturization process and travel through time. You haven't been miniaturized at all. So what's going on?"

"I have limited information with which to work," said Hunter. "However, I surmise that some of my atoms have been made similarly unstable by the repeated trips I have taken. Trauma from the spear has destroyed the shielding on a specific location in my shoulder. The unstable atoms in that area are the ones that will explode in the particle shower if I return."

"You mean this is the opposite problem of the component robots," said Steve. "They can go home safely in the particle shower, but they'll explode if they go through time normally to reach the moment they left. You're saying you can't use the belt unit, but you could wait around for hundreds of years safely?"

"That is correct."

"Well . . . can't we shield it again? Maybe MC 6 can handle the precision required."

"That should be possible," said Hunter. "I can direct him continuously by radio as he works."

"So that's what you want to do?" Steve asked quietly. He did not want to lose Hunter, but he understood that arguing with him about the Laws of Robotics was a waste of time.

"Not yet. I want to hear Jane's expertise as a roboticist. As I said, I am working with limited information. I may be wrong. If so, then my parts might explode with nuclear force when they reach the time I left on our current mission, as the component robots have."

"Maybe MC 6 can understand the damage."

"Telling him is important in any case; even Jane would only understand the principles, not retain all the precise numbers. If I sustain further damage or energy loss, this information should be available elsewhere."

Steve turned to MC 6. "Listen to everything he says and remember it."

"Acknowledged," said MC 6.

"I am transferring the data by radio link rather than speech," said Hunter. "It will be much faster. In fact, we are finished."

"Look, Hunter, can you get up and move? The only visible damage is in your shoulder. Do your legs work?"

"Technically, yes. Most of my body remains mechanically sound. However, a number of electrical circuits have been broken, some of which normally access my energy storage. I am able to reroute only minimal energy. While I might be able to walk upright for a short distance, the danger of falling and causing greater trauma is high."

"You shouldn't move."

"Not if I can avoid it."

"I see. MC 6, I want to talk about you," said Steve. "Shut down your hearing and vision. I'll have Hunter radio you to turn them on again; when he conveys my message, it will also have Second Law force."

"Acknowledged," said MC 6.

"Can we really trust MC 6 to make your repairs?" Steve asked. "What if he makes some interpretation of the First Law on his own without telling us and sabotages you? Then we'll all be stuck here."

"That is the clinching argument we need that he must cooperate," said Hunter. "The First Law will neither allow him to change history nor to harm you, Wayne, and Jane by stranding you. He must repair my condition so that we can all go back."

"All right. We have to make sure you and MC 6 are safe, then. And I still have to get Jane away from Wayne somehow."

"We must also return for Harriet," said Hunter. "First, however, I must warn you that I hear Wayne's footsteps approaching to your left, in the trees about nine meters away. From my position here on the ground, I cannot see him."

Steve turned to look. Wayne stopped warily in the trees, watching him. He had picked up a Saxon sword and shield, probably from a fresh corpse.

"Hunter, shut down your hearing and vision." Steve forced his voice to remain calm. "Turn them back on when I tap you on the arm three times quickly."

"I cannot. Danger is present. Under the First Law, I must be able to help."

"You can't help, anyway," said Steve. "Not now. And I have a chance to complete our mission."

"How?"

"Never mind how. I can do this more efficiently if I don't have to worry about you interfering. Do it."

"Is a First Law imperative involved?"

"If I complete our mission, then the First Law danger to the whole line of history to come will be finished. Now shut up and do it."

Hunter said nothing more.

Steve realized, belatedly, that ordering Hunter to shut up meant that the big robot would not acknowledge whether or not he had agreed to shut down his hearing and vision.

"If you still hear me, say so," said Steve.

Hunter still said nothing.

Steve looked through the trees at Wayne again. Obviously, Wayne had come prepared to fight if necessary. Steve decided that Wayne must have ordered Ishihara to take Jane far enough away so that the robot would not realize Wayne intended to risk getting into a fight. Wayne had seen Hunter go down with a spear in his shoulder and Wayne could control MC 6 under the Second Law. That meant he had come to fight Steve.

Wayne walked toward him slowly, still watching the robots.

Slowly, Steve drew his sword from his belt and shifted his shield on his arm to make it more comfortable. He doubted that Wayne would be any match for him in hand-to-hand combat; after all, Wayne worked in offices and laboratories as a roboticist. Steve was younger, in better shape, and had practiced with his sword and shield in Lucius's troop.

Wayne had not taken a helmet. His head remained bare. As he approached, a light breeze tossed his hair slightly.

Seeing that Wayne had neither a helmet nor any armor, Steve realized his own disadvantage. He really did not want to hurt Wayne. That did not mean he could expect the same consideration in return.

Wayne stopped about three meters away. He watched Steve silently for a moment. Then he glanced again at the motionless robots.

"Hi, Wayne." Steve grinned and spoke casually, as though nothing unusual was about to happen.

Wayne scowled. "Are they really going to let us fight? I see Hunter can't help you, but what about MC 6?"

"I told MC 6 to shut down his sight and hearing so I could talk to Hunter. And that's the way we want it. If he interfered with us, he might also get away again. But we don't have to fight. Let's talk about this for a change."

"Forget it. Step aside and let me have my own creation."

"You know I can't. Why don't you and Jane help me take care of Hunter? I don't think anybody wants to ruin your career. Hunter can help you work out the situation with the Oversight Committee."

Wayne's face contorted with anger. He raised his sword and ran at Steve.

Startled by the suddenness of Wayne's mood shift, Steve raised his shield just in time to take a hard sword blow. The power of it hurt his arm and he felt a surge of excitement. In return, he swung his own sword in a high, downward slash.

Wayne blocked the swing with his own shield, shifting to Steve's left. They exchanged rhythmic blows, each one catching the other's sword on his shield. Wayne kept moving to one side, toward MC 6, and Steve shuffled laterally to stay between them.

Steve realized that this could go on for a long time. Wayne would eventually tire before he would, but Steve did not want to wait. If anyone else came back this way, most likely Artorius's riders, the entire situation would become harder to handle.

Wayne swung his sword another time, the same way he had done before. Steve caught it on his shield again. Instead of just swinging his own, however, Steve planted his feet and took another step forward, shoving his shield outward like a weapon itself.

Caught by surprise, Wayne stumbled backward. His arms flailed out to each side as he tried to get his balance. He was momentarily exposed.

Steve raised his sword high, but brought it down with the butt end of the handle first. He hit Wayne on the top of the head with the pommel, as hard as he dared. Then he dropped his sword and pushed Wayne with his free hand.

Wayne fell onto his back. Steve wrenched the sword out of his hand and tossed it away. Then he made a fist, ready to punch Wayne if necessary.

When Steve saw Wayne lying limply on the grass, he relaxed slightly.

"How's your head?" Steve asked cautiously.

"Leave me alone," Wayne muttered, wincing. He made no move to get up.

Steve decided Wayne was not seriously injured. He stood up and dropped his shield on the ground. Then he picked up both swords and jogged back to Hunter so that Wayne could not reach the swords by a sudden move. Steve dropped the swords on the ground and tapped Hunter on the arm three times.

"I have turned on my hearing and vision again," said Hunter. "What has transpired?"

"Good news," said Steve. "Wayne is lying nearby with a minor headache. MC 6 remains in custody; instruct him to turn on his senses again."

"I am fully functional again," MC 6 said almost immediately.

"Listen carefully," said Steve. "Hunter, explain to him all the First Law imperatives involved in the danger of changing history. Do it fast, by radio again."

"Done," said Hunter.

"You agree this is a serious First Law problem?" Steve asked MC 6.

"Yes."

"Then I instruct you, with that First Law imperative in mind, to help me gather everyone who has come to this time from our own and take them back safely. Acknowledge."

"Acknowledged."

"Go see if Wayne Nystrom, over there, needs any first aid. Don't let him get away, though. Keep him here with us."

MC 6 jogged over to Wayne.

"Hunter, call Ishihara. If he answers, tell him that Wayne has been slightly hurt and that he and MC 6 are both in our custody. Wayne's mission has ended, so Ishihara's First Law imperative now is to bring Jane back to us."

"Ishihara has responded. I am conveying your mission as I speak to you. He agrees, pending his judgment that we have told the truth."

"What's he going to do?"

"He will approach cautiously. Once he sees that we have Wayne and MC 6 with us, he will be convinced."

Steve could not hear any more sounds from the battle. "Hunter, can you hear the battle? Is it still going on?"

"I hear distant hoofbeats, most of them still scattering away from us. Most of the riders are pursuing their fleeing enemy. A few have regrouped. Artorius clearly won another victory. No one is near except for the footsteps of Ishihara and the hoofbeats of the mule, about ten meters behind you."

Steve turned and saw Jane riding the mule next to Ishihara. Deciding that Hunter was safe for the moment, Steve ran toward Jane. She slipped off the mule, landing on her feet in front of him. He started to throw his arms around her, but was not sure he should, so he stopped.

"So, you're safe," he said, feeling awkward.

"Yeah." She laughed, looking at him expectantly for a moment. Then she looked past him to Hunter. "Ishihara relayed Hunter's report of his condition."

"MC 6 says he can shield the problem area, whatever it is." Steve glanced over her shoulder at Ishihara. "Are you sure of Ishihara's loyalty now?"

"Yes. I grilled him on the subject when he told me that you and Hunter had Wayne and MC 6."

"Okay. You'd know better than I would."

"I will help everyone return safely," said Ishihara. "However, I hope that Wayne's career is not destroyed. That would harm him."

"No one has ever wanted that to happen," said Jane.

Wayne pushed himself up to a sitting position, rubbing the top of his head where Steve had hit him. MC 6 stood over him. They both looked at Ishihara and Jane.

"Ishihara, MC 6 must make a repair for Hunter," said Jane. "If we can trust you not to accept any arguments from Wayne about the First Law, then I can allow you to watch over him."

"Aw, shut up," Wayne muttered. "I've had enough. You got MC 6 and all the rest of them. I just want to go home."

"Well, Ishihara?" Jane demanded. "Acknowledge that our First Law arguments supersede anything Wayne has ever told you."

"Under the new conditions that pertain, I acknowledge this."

"Good."

"You stay with Wayne, then," said Steve. "MC 6, come over to Hunter and make the repairs in communication with him."

"Yes," said MC 6, joining them.

"Are you going to need tools of any kind?" Jane asked.

"I will have to fashion some sort of precision tools," said MC 6. He knelt by Hunter and moved aside a fold of Hunter's tunic to examine the damage to Hunter's shoulder. "I can use some material from Hunter's body that has already been rendered waste matter by the damage."

"Go ahead," said Jane. "On your own judgment."

"We will confer by radio link," said Hunter.

Steve sat down next to MC 6, giving him plenty of room to move his arms as necessary. Jane sat down on his other side. They watched in silence as MC 6 carefully drew out a very thin piece of wire from Hunter's wound and shaped it with his fingers. Then he picked up a slightly heavier piece of wire and shaped it, also. After that, he used them to manipulate tiny components inside Hunter's shoulder; Steve did not know what any of them were.

Finally MC 6 drew out the small wires and neatly

rolled them. After that, he fastened them inside the wound. Then he moved the tunic back into place.

"The shielding is complete," said Hunter. "However, he found that many of my broken circuits cannot be quickly repaired, so my energy level remains minimal. I am still unable to move around without danger to myself."

"But we can all go home now, right?" Steve asked. "We'll get MC 6 back, have you fixed, then return for Harriet."

"Please go directly to Harriet with Ishihara," said Hunter. "I can hear the baggage train moving up on the road; that means tonight's camp will be made forward of this position. Jane and MC 6 can tend to Wayne and me safely in this location for a short time. I prefer to complete this mission all at once. You can use the belt unit that Ishihara carries. I will have him set it for Cadbury."

"All right. You're the boss."

"I am communicating with Ishihara now as you and I speak. However, I must emphasize to you that Harriet must come back. Her continuing presence endangers the future. I have explained by radio to Ishihara that he must bring her by force if necessary."

"I'll go baby-sit Wayne and send Ishihara over here," said Jane. She got up and walked back to them.

"All right." Steve accepted the belt unit from him. "We aren't going to see Bedwyr again, are we?"

"No. He will assume that we were killed in battle."

"Too bad. I like him."

"The mule cannot be taken back to Emrys either," said Ishihara, as he walked up.

"Who?" Steve asked.

"The owner of the mule, who loaned it to us. However, this may equalize the value of labor I contributed to him. Loss of the mule would in that case mean that our presence made less of a total change in his life."

"Please get Harriet," said Hunter. "Ishihara, when she has joined you, return here only a moment after you left. We will be safe here that long."

"You do it." Steve moved a few steps away from Hunter and handed Ishihara the belt unit.

"Ready?"

"Yes."

Harriet followed Gwenhyvaer through the narrow streets of the village again, looking at the same wares they had seen before. As Gwenhyvaer fingered the material of a woolen scarf, Harriet turned and gazed out the open gate of the village, across the front slope of the tor toward the rolling hills in the distance. She wondered how the campaign was going, though of course she knew who would win in the end. When she got a moment alone, she would call Hunter and see if her lapel pin could still reach him.

The lower level of material comfort here did not bother Harriet. She enjoyed the simple life and the lack of stress. However, in only a few days, the company she kept had begun to bore her.

As a historian, Harriet had pursued her professional research and taught a variety of classes. She had debated historical theories about Arthur both in serious professional forums and also casually with friends in other fields. Now she had found that none of the women around her had the slightest interest in the evolution of societies and values, let alone a desire to hear Harriet discuss them.

Gwenhyvaer talked constantly of her desire to marry Artorius, to assure herself of what status and privilege she could find. She and the other women here had a tremendous stake in Artorius's military successes, but otherwise they cared nothing for the details. Today, Gwenhyvaer, who in legend would become the beautiful but tragically flawed queen of Camelot, had screamed at a young servant girl for spilling mutton stew on her dress. Now her biggest concern in life was whether to buy another now or to wait until Artorius came home victorious from his campaign.

Harriet no longer wanted to spend the rest of her life in this intellectual void.

As she looked out the main gate, Steve and a man she did not know walked through it.

"Harriet!" Steve ran to her, grinning.

"You're back! But . . . I didn't see the army ride back."

Steve lowered his voice. "My friend here is Ishihara. Everything's under control, including him; the others are waiting for us near the battlefield."

"You came back just to get me."

"Well, yeah. I'm afraid Hunter insisted. Are you willing to come home?"

"Yes, I'm ready."

"You are?" Steve's eyebrows shot up in surprise.

"Yes." Harriet turned to look once more at Gwenhyvaer, who still had her back turned. "Gwenhyvaer."

"Mm?" The young woman glanced back over her shoulder.

"I'm going to take a quick walk out the gate. All right?"

"Of course." Gwenhyvaer shrugged and turned her attention back to the wares in front of her.

"Good thing she didn't notice me," Steve muttered, as they walked toward the gate. "She might wonder how I got back from the campaign so fast, when no one else has."

"I'm afraid she's quite busy with a worry of her own," Harriet said quietly, smiling. "I suppose she'll wonder what happened to me, but now that I know her, I don't think she'll wonder long."

"What? Why not?" Steve asked.

"Let's just say she is rather self-consumed."

As soon as they passed through the main gate, Ishihara pointed to a couple of trees. "That is where Steve and I arrived. No one noticed us. We will jump back from there, as well."

Steve tumbled to the grass near Hunter and MC 6. Hunter still lay where he had fallen, but Wayne was now standing with Jane. Next to Steve, Ishihara caught Harriet's arm to stop her from falling.

Hunter looked up. "All is well?"

"Yes, Hunter," said Harriet with a wry smile. "I'm ready to go home. I didn't give them any trouble."

"We must go promptly, then," said Hunter. "I hear the footsteps of the camp followers coming up the road. We do not want to be seen by them. Please leave behind whatever you can from this time period. I will confer directly with Ishihara and MC 6 so they can take off my cap and my leather armor."

The other two robots carefully crouched by Hunter to perform those chores.

Steve had already dropped his sword and shield. He took off his steel cap and tossed it down. Then he unlaced his leather armor and pulled it up over his head, to leave with the cap.

Jane took Wayne's arm and escorted him to the group. Wayne scowled at the ground but allowed Jane to bring him to a spot next to Hunter. Ishihara and MC 6 also joined them, making room for Harriet. Steve stood next to MC 6.

Hunter reached inside his tunic for his own belt unit. "Now."

Hunter felt himself jammed between Ishihara and MC 6 in the dark sphere. Ishihara and MC 6 quickly opened the crowded sphere and helped the humans climb out first. Then they carefully lifted out Hunter and laid him on the couch across the room. Hunter observed that Daladier recognized Wayne and watched him carefully, aware of Hunter's instructions to make sure Wayne remained in custody.

Steve waited uncertainly, watching Wayne also.

"Robots are so logical," said Jane. "That's what I like about them. They don't bear grudges. Now that Ishihara no longer selects his actions under Wayne's First Law argument, he's perfectly willing to help Hunter and the rest of us."

"I used to appreciate that quality in them myself," said Wayne, in a resigned tone. "Now I'm not so sure."

Jane smiled gently. "Well, I don't need to bear a grudge, either. I'm just glad we're all home again."

Wayne said nothing.

Hunter saw by Steve's scowl that he did not feel as charitable toward Wayne. Still, Steve said nothing to provoke the roboticist. Hunter had figured out that Steve had hit Wayne over the head and surmised that this had given Steve some personal satisfaction.

"Daladier," said Hunter. "Wayne should go promptly to a hospital to be examined. Please keep him in your custody."

"Of course." Daladier took Wayne's arm. "I am calling for a Medical vehicle to meet us outside right away."

"I'm not hurt bad, but I could use something for a headache," Wayne said as he walked out of the room with Daladier.

"I will call for a Security vehicle to take the rest of us to MC Governor's office," said Hunter. On his internal system, he did so. He also contacted the city computer and instructed it to reach the members of the Governor Robot Oversight Committee for a conference call.

"You need repair worse than Wayne needs a Medical robot," said Jane. "You want to arrange it right away?"

"First I must complete my mission," said Hunter.

"I thought you'd say that. All right. Ishihara, MC 6, can you carry Hunter out to the Security vehicle in front without damaging him further?"

"Yes," said Ishihara.

"I'll bring our regular clothes," said Harriet. "We can all change somewhere else."

"I'll help you with them," said Steve.

"Let's go," said Jane.

The ride through the calm city streets to MC Governor's office was uneventful. Hunter said nothing at first, monitoring the news as he rode. Steve sat near him.

"Are you checking the news?" Steve asked. "Is everything okay?"

"Yes," Hunter said quietly. "I hear no sign that any of the nuclear explosions ever took place. We have completed our mission successfully, but we have some matters to clear up. I still have to answer to the Oversight Committee, but the First Law will not allow me to permit the revelation of time travel to humanity at large."

"What about all the historians? They already know. And they aren't bound by the Laws of Robotics."

"I must confer with them, too."

"For that matter, what about Jane and me? We humans are notoriously unreliable."

"We will discuss it."

At MC Governor's office, Ishihara and MC 6 carried Hunter inside, where they carefully positioned him in the desk chair. The Security detail remained on duty just outside the door. Steve followed Jane and Harriet inside and closed the door.

"Jane," said Hunter. "Please give MC 6 instructions to merge with the other component robots to form Mojave Center Governor and make him functional again. Make sure that he remains under control, of course."

"Of course. MC 6, merge with the others as Hunter has said. As soon as your merging is complete, have MC Governor become fully functional but alert for a discussion regarding the First Law. I am instructing you not to allow MC Governor to do anything other than listen to us."

"Acknowledged." MC 6 walked over to the figure formed by the other five gestalt robots. He made contact, then fluidly slid right into place, his own physical shape altering slightly.

As Hunter watched from his chair, the entire figure smoothly became one large robot.

"I am Mojave Center Governor," he said.

"You have access to the data from each of your components?" Jane asked.

"Yes. From my combined data from each component robot, I already know all of you and what has happened."

"Good," said Hunter. "From what I overheard when Wayne spoke to MC 1 in the Late Cretaceous, you—as MC Governor—were in danger of entering an endless loop that rendered the other Governor robots helpless. Are you aware of this problem?"

"Yes," said MC Governor.

"Can you avoid going into this loop?"

"Strictly by my own choice, I believe I cannot. This is the reason I divided and fled."

"If you are given sufficient instructions under the Second Law, can you avoid it?"

"I estimate that I can. The attraction of this addiction is that it simulates constant First Law imperatives that I can satisfy."

"I understand," said Hunter. "Jane, can you give him a real First Law imperative that will override such simulations?"

"No. Now that he's been relieved of his duties here in the city and remains in our custody, his internal actions can't endanger humans or prevent harm to them. No First Law imperative regarding his thoughts alone now exists."

"Then give him whatever pertinent Second Law instructions you can."

"Listen and obey me fully," said Jane. "Do not

leave this room except under specific instruction from one of us. Do not run any simulation programs. Running them as practice for genuine First Law imperatives is not a real First Law matter, so my instructions under the Second Law take precedence. Do you acknowledge this?"

"I remain undecided," said MC Governor. "Honing my responses to First Law imperatives may still help me follow the First Law at some point in the future. However, your Second Law instructions are sufficient for me to avoid the simulations in the short term."

"All right. Then avoid any activity that would lead you to go into the simulation. Occupy your attention now by calculating the value of pi, but remain alert for one of the humans here to give you further orders. As a final instruction, do not reveal the existence of time travel. A fundamental First Law danger to all of humanity will result from humans going back into the past in large numbers. Acknowledge that the First Law prohibits you from revealing time travel."

"Acknowledged."

"Good. Begin your calculation of pi."

"Value of what?" Steve asked. "What's that supposed to accomplish?"

"Remember pi, from geometry?" Harriet said quietly. "It's an endless calculation. It'll just keep him busy."

"Oh, yeah. Geometry."

"Hunter," said Harriet. "I think my usefulness to you really ended quite a long time ago. If you don't mind, I'd like to return to my hotel room."

"Of course. Please stand by, however, for a conference call among all our specialists—one paleontologist and five historians. I will be arranging it shortly."

"All right." Harriet turned to Steve. "I'm sorry I wasn't more of a help, but I'm glad everything worked out."

"You had the information we needed when we needed it," said Steve. "No need to apologize."

Harriet said good-bye to everyone and left.

"City computer calling Hunter. The conference call you requested is standing by."

"Connect me. Also contact the six specialists I have hired for a similar conference call." Hunter called Daladier on a different band and communicated at maximum robotic speed.

"Daladier here."

"How is Wayne? Give me your location."

"Wayne will be fine. The Medical robots have just completed diagnostic tests and found no significant injury. They have provided a mild painkiller and we are now walking down a hall toward the main door of the clinic."

"I want Wayne to observe a conference call with the Oversight Committee. Have you seen any video screens that I can link?"

"Yes. The main lobby has a large screen."

"Wait in the lobby and have Wayne observe the call." Hunter contacted the city computer again and instructed it to send the conference call to the screen in the clinic lobby.

At the same moment, the four members of the Oversight Committee appeared on his internal screens.

"Yes, Hunter?" Dr. Redfield, the blonde, smiled hopefully. "Does this mean your mission has been completed?"

"Yes, it does," said Hunter. He waited while Dr. Redfield, Dr. Chin, Dr. Khanna, and Professor Post congratulated him. "I also have good news to report. From the preliminary explanation of the flaw in the gestalt robots, I expect the problem can be eliminated without destroying the memories or identities of the component robots or the Governors. Unless presently unforeseeable problems appear during later examination, their system programming will simply have to include a more narrowly defined set of priorities involving First Law interpretations."

"That's excellent," said Dr. Chin, tossing her black hair. "It means the problem is not as difficult as we expected."

"That's right," said Professor Post, stroking his black beard. "The Governors will not have to be destroyed."

"Surely the time has come for a preliminary report, Hunter," said Dr. Khanna. "You have done very well. But with your mission completed, I ask you in full expectation of an answer: Where did you find the component robots, and under what circumstances?"

Hunter had always known this moment would arrive. His interpretation of the First Law and his judgment of human frailty prevented him from revealing the existence of time travel. He also felt that revealing Wayne's obstruction of the mission would, in fact, bring about consequences that would harm Wayne. Now that Hunter had completed the mission successfully, he saw no reason to allow such harm. None of Wayne's illegal actions in the past, such as kidnapping Jane, could be proven in a contemporary court of law, so legal action was not an option. Hunter decided to delete information about Wayne's presence on these missions.

"The First Law prohibits me from giving a detailed report," Hunter said in a formal tone.

"This is an unacceptable answer," Dr. Khanna said angrily. "You have put me off at every request. As the Oversight Committee, we have a right to this information."

"The First Law makes no exceptions," said Hunter.

Dr. Khanna drew in a long breath, his face contorted with anger. Before he could speak again, however, he was interrupted.

"That's true," said Dr. Redfield, stifling a smile. "We're all roboticists here. Apparently Hunter has no choice."

"I question his judgment on this matter," Dr. Khanna said with barely controlled rage. "Must we dismantle Hunter to make sure of his efficiency?"

"He reports that he's completed his assignment successfully," said Dr. Redfield. "If that turns out to be true, then we have no real grounds to question him."

"I will have MC Governor shut down and will arrange for him to be shipped to a lab of your choice," said Hunter.

"We have to make arrangements first," said Dr. Chin. "We'll contact you when we are ready."

"I suggest we confer among ourselves," said Professor Post. "We should have Hunter sign off."

"I must ask a question," said Hunter. "Where does Dr. Wayne Nystrom stand in regard to your deliberations?"

"Nobody can stand him," Dr. Khanna said, still angry.

"That's a personal matter," said Professor Post. "In professional terms, Dr. Nystrom will have to face a detailed review of his flawed creations."

"Can you utilize his expertise in your upcoming research?" Hunter asked.

"Our oversight responsibility must be conducted without conflict of interest," said Dr. Redfield. "However, once our judgment of existing flaws has been reached, that phase will have ended. When the repair process begins, we can consider contacting him for help."

"Do you have a recommendation, Hunter?" Dr. Chin asked. "Why do you ask?"

"I will discuss a possible suggestion with you at a later time," said Hunter. "I will sign off now."

"Thanks for a great job," Dr. Redfield added, just before the connection broke.

Without stopping to speak with the humans in MC Governor's office, Hunter called Daladier again. "Did Wayne observe this call successfully?"

"Yes."

"Is there a phone nearby? I want to speak with him directly."

"Yes." Daladier gave Hunter a number to call. "It's right here in the lobby. I will tell Wayne to answer."

Hunter called the number. A moment later, Wayne's face appeared on Hunter's internal screen.

"Yeah?" Wayne said cautiously, glaring at Hunter.

"You are well?" Hunter asked.

"Well enough. Get to the point, will you?"

"Based on the reaction of the Oversight Committee, I believe the members will consider your participation in correcting the flaws of the Governor robots."

"Dr. Khanna never liked me. And the feeling's mutual. They're all jealous of my accomplishments."

"If you are willing to participate, I believe they will work with you. In that event, your career may not be significantly harmed."

Wayne said nothing for a moment, looking at Hunter. "Yeah?"

"I will offer you a deal in exchange for my recommending to the Oversight Committee that they ask for your help in the repair process."

"How do you know they'll bother to repair the Governor robots?" Wayne asked, in a less confrontational tone. "I always figured they'd just junk them entirely."

"I cannot speak for them," said Hunter. "But Dr. Redfield raised the subject of a repair phase on her own. The Oversight Committee appears to have an open mind on the subject."

"Well, yeah, I heard her mention that," Wayne said slowly. "What do you want from me in return?"

"I want you to keep the existence of time travel a secret. The inherent harm to all humans is clearly immense."

"Yeah, I know that. But what about the hardware?"

"The First Law will not allow me to discuss my plans. However, I offer the proposition that if no evidence of time travel continues to exist, anyone claiming to have visited the past will sound silly, not to mention professionally unreliable."

Wayne hesitated, then nodded. "I hear the implied threat to my own future, Hunter. All right, you have a deal."

"Good. You can find lodging in Mojave Center for the time being?"

"Yes."

"Excellent. Feel free to have Daladier continue

to assist you. I will confer with you again later. Hunter out."

"Hunter, city computer calling. The second conference call you requested stands by."

"Please connect me."

"Hunter, is everything okay?" Jane asked.

"Yes," Hunter said aloud. "Jane, and Steve, please stand by. In a moment, we will return to the Bohung Institute."

"Okay," said Steve.

As the six specialists appeared on Hunter's internal link, he greeted each one of them.

"What's up, Hunter?" Chad Mora, the paleontologist who had helped find MC 1 in the Late Cretaceous era, grinned at him. "You don't have to find another robot in the age of dinosaurs, do you?"

"No. We have completed our missions."

A chorus of congratulations came from all of them except Harriet, who of course already knew that.

"I'm glad, Hunter," said Rita Chavez, who had journeyed to Jamaica in the time of the buccaneers with the team.

"I want to thank you again, Hunter," said Gene Titus. "For inviting me along to Roman Germany. It was a wonderful experience for a historian; I guess we all feel that way."

"That's right," said Judy Taub, who had traveled back to the Battle of Moscow in 1941 with the team.

"I still can't believe I met Marco Polo and Kublai Khan," said Marcia Lew.

"Have any of you revealed that you traveled into the past?"

No one responded; several shook their heads.

"It's been less than a week," said Chad. "I'm still reviewing all the information I collected."

"We all know the danger of revealing time travel to the world at large," said Judy.

"I made significant discoveries," said Harriet. "I may not be alone in that. But I know you want us to keep this a secret."

"I will dismantle the time-travel ability of the sphere shortly," said Hunter. "Of course, I cannot order you to keep this a secret. I can tell you that no evidence of time travel will exist, however. Certainly none of us will benefit by having the technology rediscovered."

"I get the picture," said Chad. "If we claim to have traveled through time, we'll sound like cranks or lunatics."

"As you know, I cannot allow harm to any of you," said Hunter. "So I want you to know that maintaining the secret will be to your own advantage."

"I can manage," said Harriet. "Even though I can't prove my information, I know where to pursue more archaeological research. Maybe I can arrange it."

"I can, too," said Chad. "Paleontology combines hard evidence with educated guesses all the time. I can advance my new information as theoretical. Since I'm right, no one can disprove it." He laughed lightly. "And I know roughly where to dig next."

"I didn't learn much new history as such," said Marcia. "I picked up the feel of the times. That helps me in my work, too."

"Same for me," said Gene.

"Yes, I would say that," added Rita. "It all became real."

"I have further work to do," said Hunter. "Please excuse me for making this farewell so abrupt. I thank you all." He disconnected and turned to Steve and Jane. "We must go back to the Bohung Institute now. Jane, can we safely leave MC Governor here?"

"Yes," said Jane. "Under the Second Law, he can't violate my instruction to stay in the room and I don't believe he can come up with a First Law argument to justify overriding it."

"Especially while he's calculating pi?" Steve grinned.

"Right. Besides, Ishihara can stay here to guard him and that Security detail is still right outside. We can instruct them to stop MC Governor bodily from leaving if necessary."

"Please do that as we leave," said Hunter. "Ishihara, remain here with MC Governor. Stop him if he attempts to leave and call me immediately. Soon I can allow the Bohung Institute to reopen, at which time you may resume your normal duties. You know this situation has First Law force."

"Agreed."

"We will go."

Steve rode with Hunter and Jane in the same vehicle they had taken to MC Governor's office. Jane had given the Security detail guarding the office their instructions. Now no one spoke as Hunter drove them back through the streets of Mojave Center.

During the ride, Steve felt out of place. He had originally been hired because of his experience outdoors, to be part of a team made up of Hunter and city people. At Hunter's request, he had remained part of the team in the later missions. Now, his contribution had clearly ended. He wondered if he should say good-bye also, but he did not really want the experience to end yet. The missions had all been exciting, and he wanted to spend more time with Jane. On the other hand, he expected that she was anxious to get back home and return to her normal routine now that the job had ended.

At the Bohung Institute, they returned quickly to Room F-12. Hunter walked to the console near the sphere and opened it. As he worked inside the console, Jane stood with Steve watching.

"It's been a wild adventure," said Steve. "Or six separate ones."

"I can hardly believe we visited all those times and places," said Jane. She shook her head slowly. "And now it's over."

"We must hope so," said Hunter as he continued to work. "When I have finished, the sphere will be returned only to its original function of miniaturization for industrial and medical purposes."

"And that will be the end of time travel," said Steve.

"Only if we are unusually fortunate," said Hunter. "A technological development that is created once can be created again. Historically, this usually happens. I will impress further on all the robots who know about our missions that the First Law will not allow this technology to be restored, revealed, or discussed. Wayne and our specialists have shown no particular desire to travel in time again. Beyond that, we can only hope that this technology will be an exception that no one discovers a second time."

"But you don't think that's likely," said Steve.

"The only reason for optimism is that no one seems motivated to pursue research in this direction. Maybe that will be reason enough."

"It was a great experience for me," said Steve. "I'd forgotten just how big the world is. And a society that can make Governor robots and create Hunter and send people back in time has a lot to offer."

"Maybe I learned the opposite," Jane said quietly. "I've worked in an ivory tower of schools and research labs all my life. The world is much more than robots and technological theories."

"Yeah." Steve glanced at Hunter, who was still working on the console. "I guess my part is finished, isn't it, Hunter?"

Hunter looked up. "Yes. I asked you to accompany me here so I can return you to your home as soon as I finish."

"Right." Steve turned to Jane, feeling awkward. "Well, I guess this will be good-bye. I, uh, enjoyed working with you. A couple of times, I thought we might have a chance to get better acquainted, but then something always happened."

"We have time now." Jane smiled.

"Uh . . . don't you have to go home, or something?"

"That can wait. Would you take me up to see your shack again?"

"My shack?"

"The first time Hunter took Chad and me up there to meet you, I thought it was a weird, rickety combination of a primitive shelter and modern conveniences."

"Well . . ." Steve grinned. "I guess it is."

"After all we've been through, I think I might find it downright luxurious now."

"It's not too bad."

"I'd like to stay out in nature a little longer without having to chase robots, too. Maybe you could show me around your desert a little . . . if I'm welcome."

"Of course you are." Steve laughed. "I'd love to have you come and visit."

"I am finished here." Hunter closed the console. "And now you two no longer have to worry about changing history."

"That's right," said Steve. "Who knows? Maybe we can make our own."

AVONOVA PRESENTS
AWARD-WINNING NOVELS
FROM MASTERS OF SCIENCE FICTION

WULFSYARN
by Phillip Mann   71717-4/ $4.99 US

MIRROR TO THE SKY
by Mark S. Geston   71703-4/ $4.99 US/ $5.99 Ca

THE DESTINY MAKERS
by George Turner   71887-1/ $4.99 US/ $5.99 Ca

A DEEPER SEA
by Alexander Jablokov   71709-3/ $4.99 US/ $5.99 Ca

BEGGARS IN SPAIN
by Nancy Kress   71877-4/ $4.99 US/ $5.99 Ca

FLYING TO VALHALLA
by Charles Pellegrino   71881-2/ $4.99 US/ $5.99 Ca